BIBLE SEARCH

DISCOVERING ANSWERS IN GOD'S WORD

JON NAPPA

ILLUSTRATED BY ROB CORLEY AND TOM BANCROFT

For a free catalog
of NavPress books & Bible studies call
1-800-366-7788 (USA) or 1-800-839-4769 (Canada).

www.navpress.com

The Navigators is an international Christian organization. Our mission is to advance the gospel of Jesus and His kingdom into the nations through spiritual generations of laborers living and discipling among the lost. We see a vital movement of the gospel, fueled by prevailing prayer, flowing freely through relational networks and out into the nations where workers for the kingdom are next door to everywhere.

NavPress is the publishing ministry of The Navigators. The mission of NavPress is to reach, disciple, and equip people to know Christ and make Him known by publishing life-related materials that are biblically rooted and culturally relevant. Our vision is to stimulate spiritual transformation through every product we publish.

Creative Team: Kent Wilson, Lori Mitchell, Amy Spencer, Heather Dunn, Kris Wallen, Arvid Wallen, Darla Hightower, Pat Reinheimer
Design by studiogearbox.com
Illustrated by Rob Corley and Tom Bancroft. Colors by Jon Conkling.

ISBN-10: 1-60006-249-0
ISBN-13: 978-1-60006-249-0

Published in association with the literary agency of Leslie H. Stobbe, 300 Doubleday Road, Tryon, NC 28782.

Printed in China

1 2 3 4 5 6 7 8 9 10 / 12 11 10 09 08

CONTENTS

CONCORDANCE:

DICTIONARY:

INTRODUCTION

Welcome to a very grown-up book! Here you'll find lots of help for many of the things you'll experience in your life. Turn to any chapter, and you'll see each idea explained in easy-to-understand ways. Then you'll find Scriptures that will help and encourage you. There will also be fun things to do and places to write what you're thinking and learning.

You'll see that this book is divided into two parts: a concordance and a dictionary. They're both very fun. The concordance talks about things you'll experience in your life and how to deal with them in a grown-up and biblical way. The dictionary will help you know what some words mean.

Did you see the fun pictures? Manty and lots of the other characters from the *My First Message* Bible are here to give you clues about each chapter. And, boy, are there a lot of chapters! Don't try to read them all at once. Just read one at a time. You don't have to read them in order either. Just pick chapters that are interesting to you. Sooner or later you'll get to all the chapters. Don't be in a hurry.

You can read this book all by yourself, with a friend, or with your mom or dad or grandma or grandpa, or even with your Sunday school teacher. There might be some parts you want to read alone. There might be other chapters you want to read with a friend who needs some help. It's always cool to read with your parents or grand-parents. Adults like talking with you and learning with you, so include them when you can.

This is a book for those who are growing up. We're proud of you for wanting to do it in a way that pleases God. In this book, you'll find lots of help figuring things out by looking at what God says. We didn't come up with anything brand-new. Everything is straight from the Bible. In fact, we want you to use this book with your Bible. This book will show you how to find help in your Bible for lots of the things you'll deal with as you grow up. It'll help you figure out what some grown-up words mean too. So, grab your Bible and have a great time.

BIBLE HELP FOR DAILY EXPERIENCES

INTRODUCTION TO THE CONCORDANCE

A concordance is a fancy way of saying, "Here's where to find something in the Bible." We've tried to take a lot of the things you're going to face as you grow up and talk with you about them. For every situation, we've given you three ways to think about what you're facing. When you read the titles at the top of each little chart, you'll most likely find one of them that makes sense to you right now. Read through what the chart says and think about it. Look up the Scriptures in your Bible. Then try doing what we suggest on the next page. You'll find lots of fun things to try as you're working on growing up.

Remember, you don't need to read all of these chapters at once. And you don't need to read them in order. You get to pick the chapter that sounds most interesting to you.

You can write in this book too. You'll find lots of places to write down how you're feeling and what you're learning. Putting these things in words can help you think them through. It will also be a good thing to keep. Later (next week, next year, or even when you're much older), you can come back to this book and remember what you learned. And if you want to write your own concordance pages, use the blank pages at the end of this section.

WHEN I'M DISCOURAGED

Stacks of homework, lists of chores, friends who are being mean, upset parents . . . these are just a few of the things that bring discouragement. Having too much to do, feeling like you aren't in control, or feeling bad about yourself all lead to discouragement.

WHERE CAN IT COME FROM?

Are you tired?

"It's too hard!" "This is taking too long!" Have you ever said either of those things? When chores or homework take a long time, sometimes you get tired and just want to give up.

Then try dividing the work into smaller parts. You can move a mountain, just not all at once. If the whole job is too big, divide the work into smaller parts. Work on getting one thing done at a time. When you get one part done, stop and celebrate for a few minutes, then start the next part. God will help you get the whole job done. Just ask him.

Scripture:
Philippians 4:13
You can do it with God's help.

Are you worried?

Do you sometimes spend lots of time worrying about things that might happen? Sometimes they do happen, sometimes they don't. But worrying about them won't help a bit—and it just makes you discouraged.

Then try remembering God. Hey, who is in control? Well, it isn't you. Or your friends. And not even your parents. God is in control. The best way to fight the worry that brings discouragement is to trust God. You can know that he has the power to take care of everything.

Scripture:
Romans 8:28
All things can work for the good.

Did you fail at something?

Join the club! All of us fail. That means you and that means me and everyone else in the world. No one is perfect, so you're part of a big club. When you spend your time thinking about all of the times you've failed, you're going to get discouraged.

Then try admitting that you failed. Just fess up. If you did something that hurt someone, tell him or her you're sorry. If you did something wrong, tell on yourself and then fix it. Most importantly, tell God what you did and ask him to help you do the right thing next time. Whatever you did, it isn't the end of the world. We'd all be goners if it was.

Scripture:
John 3:16-17
God loves you!

CHECK OUT THIS SCRIPTURE. FIND IT IN YOUR BIBLE AND READ WHAT IT SAYS. IN ONE SENTENCE, WRITE WHAT YOU THINK IT SAYS.

Isaiah 40:28-31 _____

_____

NOW, TRY THIS IDEA.

Draw a picture of what this makes you think of. How can your picture help you the next time you get discouraged? Is there someone you know who you could help by showing them your picture and telling them about these verses?

COMPLETE THE FOLLOWING

I stopped being discouraged when I _____

_____.

From now on, when I get discouraged, I'm going to _____

_____.

Romans 8:28
Every detail in our lives of love for God is worked into something good.

WHEN I FEEL SAD

The sky is gray and so are you. You can't find anything to be happy about. You feel like there is a dark cloud floating above your head. You are just plain-old sad, and you don't even know why.

WHERE CAN IT COME FROM?

Are you bored?

Are you sad because you don't have anything to do? Maybe you don't feel useful, or you feel like no one needs you.

Then try action. The best thing to do is to get busy! Help your neighbors weed their garden. Do a chore for your parents. Play with your little brother or sister. Get busy and stop thinking about yourself so much!

Scripture:
Proverbs 13:4
Satisfaction comes from action.

Is your heart hurting?

Losing someone hurts! If it's because a friend or a loved one moved away or died, you are going to miss that person! Or maybe your pet died. Saying good-bye is never easy for anyone.

Then try letting it out. It's okay to hurt. Grieving the loss of a loved one is sad, and that's okay. Let yourself go through the process of being angry, sad, and lonely. Cry into your pillow, cry to God, and cry with a friend or family member. Facing your grief is important and will help you feel better in the long run.

Scripture:
Luke 6:21
Tears can turn to laughter.

Is life unfair?

It is hard when life doesn't go according to your plans. Maybe you have to wait for things you want right now. You might think others have more than you or that they get more attention than you.

Then try looking ahead. Oooo, this is a hard one! Unfortunately, you don't get to make all the rules in the world. Sometimes you have to wait for your turn. Your turn will come. Just keep looking ahead.

Scripture:
Romans 12:12
Patience and joy are buddies!

CHECK OUT THIS SCRIPTURE. FIND IT IN YOUR BIBLE AND READ WHAT IT SAYS. IN ONE SENTENCE, WRITE WHAT YOU THINK IT SAYS.

Matthew 6:19-21 _____

_____

NOW, TRY THIS IDEA.

Find or make a little box and turn it into your treasure chest. What will you put in it? How can these treasures help you when you're sad?

COMPLETE THE FOLLOWING

I stopped being sad when I _____

_____ .

From now on, when I get sad, I'm going to _____

_____ .

Romans 12:12
   Don't quit in hard times; pray all the harder.

WHEN I SAY THINGS I SHOULDN'T

Wow! Your mouth can really get you into trouble, can't it? How many times have you gotten into an argument or fight because of something you said? How often are you punished or grounded because of something you said? If it happens often, maybe you can change something.

WHERE CAN IT COME FROM?

Are you showing disrespect?

Did you know that the way you speak to others shows how you really feel about them? If you talk back to your parents or mouth off to your teachers, it shows that you don't have much respect for them. This is not the way to treat anyone.

Try showing honor. Remember that we are to treat others the way we want to be treated. Choose to speak in a way that shows respect for parents or teachers. In fact, speak with respect for all people, the same way you would like others to speak to you.

Scripture:
Matthew 22:36-40
Speak to others like you want them to speak to you.

Are you saying foolish things?

Do you feel like you opened your mouth and the silliest words poured out? Speaking before thinking about what you're saying can cause big problems. You're not the first person to make this mistake, and you won't be the last. But don't use this as an excuse to keep doing it.

Then try thinking before you speak. You might need to apologize for things you said before. So you don't have to apologize again, stop and think about your words, about how they sound and how they will make others feel. Always think before you speak.

Scripture:
Proverbs 29:11
Holding back is helpful and smart!

Are you using bad words?

There are some words that we shouldn't say. Sometimes we hear them and don't realize they're bad. But sometimes we do know they're bad, and when we say them, we feel dirty or mean.

Then try keeping bad words out. The only words that can come out of your mouth are the ones you've let into your brain. Think about how those words got into your brain, and then do things to keep them out. If that means watching different TV or choosing different music or hanging out with different friends, do that.

Scripture:
Psalm 19:14
Speak right words!

CHECK OUT THIS SCRIPTURE. FIND IT IN YOUR BIBLE AND READ WHAT IT SAYS. IN ONE SENTENCE, WRITE WHAT YOU THINK IT SAYS.

James 3:3-10_____

_____

NOW, TRY THIS IDEA.

Ask your mom or dad for a paper plate and fold it in half so it looks like a mouth with a big smile. Draw lips around the outside with a red marker and then add a tongue inside. Use your mouth puppet to tell your favorite story. Think about how your mouth is like that puppet. Can it tell a story without your help or if its lips are closed? How else can remembering this silly mouth puppet help you tame your tongue?

COMPLETE THE FOLLOWING

I tamed my tongue by _____

_____ .

From now on, I'm going to watch what I say because _____

_____ .

Proverbs 29:11
A fool lets it all hang out.

WHEN I GET REALLY MAD

Do you ever want to hit someone or throw something or yell and shout? There are lots of things in life that make us mad. Sometimes things just aren't fair. Sometimes people hurt your feelings. Other times you're just having a bad day. Being mad isn't always wrong, but you always need to be careful how you act.

WHERE CAN IT COME FROM?

Are there lots of little things?

When little things add up, it can make a big thing. If people around you are fighting and things aren't going well at school, they add up and make you mad. If you lost your lunch money and forgot your homework and then a friend says one wrong thing, you get mad.

Then try looking at things one at a time. Don't let things build up. If something is bugging you, talk about it. If you're having a problem, ask for help. God is always willing to help you. And he has given you friends and family and teachers too.

Scripture:
Psalm 55:22
God will help you.

Are your feelings hurt?

Did you have a fight with your friend or mom or dad or brother or sister? Did someone say something mean? These things are going to happen. Unkind or angry words from others hurt our feelings.

Then try having a talk, first with God and then with the person who hurt your feelings. Fill up with God's love and then offer that love to your friend or family member. Having a cry in your pillow or just giving it a few punches won't hurt either.

Scripture:
Proverbs 15:1
Gentle answers make things better.

Is someone being mean?

Has someone really hurt you? Do you have bumps and bruises? Does someone yell at you often or scare you? These things sure can make you mad!

Then try getting some help. Talk to a safe person about what is happening. Hiding hurts only makes things worse. Be honest with your safe person. God wants to comfort his children when they hurt.

Scripture:
Psalm 46:1
God will always help.

Proverbs 30:33 _____

_____

NOW, TRY THIS IDEA.

Try turning your anger into something good. Clean your room, rake some leaves, shovel some snow, shoot some hoops. Every time you pick up something in your room or shoot a hoop, give a part of your anger to God. Keep going until you're not mad anymore.

COMPLETE THE FOLLOWING

I got over being mad when I _____

_____ .

From now on, instead of getting mad, I'm going to _____

_____ .

James 1:19
Lead with your ears, follow up with your tongue, and let anger straggle along in the rear.

WHEN I'M CRITICAL OF OTHERS

Being critical of others means you're judging how they act or think. Do you pick on your little brother or sister? Do you make fun of the way someone looks? Do you tease others about how they do things or how they walk, talk, or breathe? If you do, then you're being critical. How do you suppose that person feels?

WHERE CAN IT COME FROM?

Are you quick to judge?

Making a decision from a little bit of information leads to big mistakes. It also means that someone's feelings are going to be hurt because they've been judged unfairly.

Then try getting the facts. Slow down and get all the facts about a situation or a person before you form an opinion. Give your friends a chance. Be kind and understanding.

Scripture:
James 2:12-13
Mercy is stronger than judgment.

Are you looking wrongly?

Do you look at other people more carefully than yourself? Do you think that you *never* make mistakes? Are you sure? Maybe you're concentrating more on what other people do than on what you do.

Then try looking at yourself first. No one is perfect. Be honest with yourself and remember that you sometimes make bad choices and mistakes. We all do! Remember to cut your friends and family a little slack and forgive them when they make mistakes, just like you want them to forgive you.

Scripture:
Matthew 7:3-5
Consider your own mistakes.

Are you being mean?

Sometimes we do things because we don't like someone. Are you being mean to someone because you don't like him or her? What are you saying and how are you saying things to those around you?

Then try loving others. Ask God to help you see the good in others, and talk about those things. Think about how you want others to treat you.

Scripture:
Luke 6:31
Treat others how you want to be treated.

CHECK OUT THIS SCRIPTURE. FIND IT IN YOUR BIBLE AND READ WHAT IT SAYS. IN ONE SENTENCE, WRITE WHAT YOU THINK IT SAYS.

Philippians 4:8 _____

_____

NOW, TRY THIS IDEA.

Think of something good about every person in your family.
Go and tell each person what you thought of.

COMPLETE THE FOLLOWING

I stopped being critical of others when I _____
_____ .

From now on, instead of being critical of others, I'm going to _____
_____ .

Matthew 7:1
 Don't pick on people, jump on their failures, criticize their faults.

WHEN OTHERS SEEM BETTER THAN ME

Does it feels like everyone is better than you at math or soccer? Maybe it feels like your friend is better at drawing or reading. No one is the best at everything. God made you to be really good at something, but not everything.

WHERE CAN IT COME FROM?

Are you jealous?

Jealous people don't want anyone to be better than they are. Are you unhappy when others do well? Do you want to be like someone else instead of yourself?

Then try looking at what you do well and be happy about that. When you're happy about yourself and about how God made you, you can look at others and be happy for them. God has given everyone special gifts and talents. Be happy, because everyone has a part to play on God's team.

Scripture:
1 Corinthians 1:7
All God's gifts are right in front of you.

Are you measuring wrongly?

Are you measuring yourself by what God made you to be or by what others are doing? When you measure yourself by looking at others, you'll never be happy.

Then try using the right measure. Remember that every person is important to God. He gave each of us work to do and the talent to do it. Think about what God has given you to do, and don't worry about others.

Scripture:
1 Corinthians 7:17
Where you are right now is God's place for you.

Are you needing to be first?

Have you ever seen a bunch of baby animals when it's time to eat? Puppies and kittens climb all over each other to get to the food first. Do you always have to be first? Is being first really important to you?

Then try taking the right place. It's good to always do your best, but don't mistake your best for being first. God always wants you to do your best. God also says that doing your best means being second or even last sometimes.

Scripture:
Mark 9:35
Take the last place. Be a servant of all.

CHECK OUT THIS SCRIPTURE. FIND IT IN YOUR BIBLE AND READ WHAT IT SAYS. IN ONE OR TWO SENTENCES, WRITE WHAT YOU THINK IT SAYS.

1 Corinthians 12:12-27 _____

_____

_____

NOW, TRY THIS IDEA.

Find some scraps of different colors of paper or just use the colorful comics from the weekend news-paper. Tear them into small pieces, and then glue them onto a plain piece of paper to make a picture of yourself. Think of how many pieces there are in your body. There are a lot of pieces in God's family just like there are a lot of pieces in you!

COMPLETE THE FOLLOWING

I stopped measuring myself with others when I _____

_____ .

From now on, instead of looking at others, I'm going to _____

_____ .

1 Corinthians 7:17
Where you are right now is God's place for you.

WHEN I SHOW OFF

Are you a person who is always showing off? Does it make others think, "Wow! You're so cool! I wish I were just like you!" Yeah, probably not. No one likes a show-off. Why do you show off?

WHERE CAN IT COME FROM?

Are you proud?

It's okay to be proud of the way God made you. If you have to tell others how great you are, though, that is a problem.

Then try being humble. All we have, all we can do, all we can think, all we will ever be, all of it is a gift from God. Do your best and when others notice, thank them. And then tell how it came from God.

Scripture:
Proverbs 18:12
Humility brings honor.

Do you need to be noticed?

All of us want to be important. Are you trying to be more important than everyone else? Do you always need to be the center of attention?

Then try being okay with attention from God. Did you know he's watching over you all the time? He's so proud of the things you do and he always notices. Listen to what God is saying to you. He wants you to know that he thinks you're wonderful!

Scripture:
Psalm 36:7
God's love is worth more than anything.

Do you like to be the clown?

Show-offs are seldom quiet, and they are often having lots of fun. There's nothing wrong with having fun or making other people laugh. Make sure you're being a clown for the right reason.

Then try thinking before you speak. It's okay to make people laugh. Be sure you're making fun of yourself and not others. If you have the gift of humor, share it with others and show them how God fills you with joy.

Scripture:
Romans 12:3
Don't think too highly of yourself.

CHECK OUT THIS SCRIPTURE. FIND IT IN YOUR BIBLE AND READ WHAT IT SAYS. IN ONE SENTENCE, WRITE WHAT YOU THINK IT SAYS.

Proverbs 20:11 _____

_____

NOW, TRY THIS IDEA.

Ask three people to tell you what they know about you. Think about what they say. Be thankful that others notice so many good things about you.

1

2

3

COMPLETE THE FOLLOWING

I decided against showing off when I _____

_____ .

From now on, instead of showing off, I'm going to _____

_____ .

James 4:6
   God goes against the willful proud; God gives grace to the willing humble.

WHEN I DON'T WANT TO GO TO BED

When your parents say, "Time for bed!" do you run to your room, pull on your jammies, brush your teeth, and jump into bed? If you don't, why not? There might be several reasons, and some of them you may never have even thought about.

WHERE CAN IT COME FROM?

Do you dislike rules?

Do you have a problem with rules? When someone tells you to do something, do you want to do the exact opposite? When you don't follow the rules, it causes lots of problems.

Then try choosing to obey. It helps to remember that rules are made for a reason. In this case, you need sleep to be able to grow and to do your best. Another cool thing is that your parents will trust you more when you show them they can trust you to obey.

Scripture:
Colossians 3:20
Obeying Mom and Dad pleases God.

Are you scared?

Are you afraid to be alone in your room at night? The dark is scary because you can't see, and what you can't see worries you. Most people don't like being alone in dark places. But you're not alone. God is there too.

Then try taking some action. Find a way to get a little light into your room. Ask for a little lamp or nightlight with cool colors. Before you turn out the lights, take a good look around so you feel good about where you are. Above all, remember that God loves you and will watch over you in your room.

Scripture:
Psalm 91:11
He commands the angels to guard you!

Are you acting spoiled?

You're spoiled if you're asking for more all of the time and expecting to get it. Staying up late to read a book, watch TV, or text a friend are fine things unless you're asking for more instead of getting the sleep you need to stay healthy.

Then try setting some limits. It's important to keep a balance in how you spend your time. When you spend too much time on one thing, something else suffers. Part of growing up is learning to set your own limits and keeping them. Give it a try. You'll be proud of yourself, and you won't be tired either.

Scripture:
Psalm 92:2
Each part of the day has something wonderful to experience.

CHECK OUT THIS SCRIPTURE. FIND IT IN YOUR BIBLE AND READ WHAT IT SAYS. IN ONE SENTENCE, WRITE WHAT YOU THINK IT SAYS.

Ephesians 6:1-3 _____

_____

NOW, TRY THIS IDEA.

Talk with your parents about your bedtime rules so you understand them. Agree to follow those rules. See if you can do it every night for five nights. See how you feel after five days.

COMPLETE THE FOLLOWING

I went to bed when asked this week because _____

_____ .

I'm going to bed on time from now on because _____

_____ .

Colossians 3:20
Do what your parents tell you. This delights the Master no end.

WHEN I DON'T WANT TO SHARE

"It's mine and you can't have it!" "Don't touch my stuff!" If you don't share, you get to keep your stuff for yourself. But will anyone want to play with you? Besides, if your friends or brother or sister have some cool stuff you'd like to try, will they want to share with you if you've never shared with them?

WHERE CAN IT COME FROM?

Are you selfish?

If you're not sharing, maybe you're thinking only of yourself and what you want. Are you forgetting that others have feelings too? Your parents share almost everything with you. Sharing is a grown-up thing to do.

Then try thinking of others. You want your friends to have fun and enjoy life as much as you, right? Sometimes that means sharing. God has given you so much, and when you share, you'll find that it actually feels good. Sharing spreads good feelings to everyone.

Scripture:
Galatians 6:10
Do good to everyone!

Are you greedy?

Are you happy with what you have, or do you always want more? If you have a new bike, but still want the one that someone else has, that's a problem.

Then try getting real. Look at what you really need. Do you really need more? Will it help anything to hold on tight to everything you have? Did you know it feels really good when you stop thinking about having more and enjoy sharing what you have with others?

Scripture:
Matthew 5:42
Give to all who ask.

Are you afraid?

Are you afraid that something will happen to your cool stuff? Are you afraid it'll get broken? It could happen. It can break if you use it or if someone else uses it.

Then try looking at the bigger picture. What's the worst that could happen? Can it be all that bad? If something breaks, it would have happened anyway, and you can get it fixed or replaced. And is it worth losing a friend over?

Scripture:
1 Timothy 6:18
Be generous and share!

CHECK OUT THIS SCRIPTURE. FIND IT IN YOUR BIBLE AND READ WHAT IT SAYS. IN ONE SENTENCE, WRITE WHAT YOU THINK IT SAYS.

John 6:5-13 _____

_____

NOW, TRY THIS IDEA.

Make a sandwich and share it with someone. Look around and see how many other things you can share today. You can share your things, your affection (hugs and stuff), or your ideas (write a note or help someone solve a problem). Then, tonight, tell God about what you learned.

COMPLETE THE FOLLOWING

I learned that sharing isn't so bad when I _____

_____ .

From now on, I'm going to share because _____

_____ .

Galatians 6:6
   [Share] all the good things that you have.

WHEN I SPEAK UNKINDLY

Saying unkind things to people makes them feel pretty rotten about themselves. It doesn't do much for your friendship either. Talking to others about their faults and problems is unkind. Reminding them of their mistakes is unkind too. Speaking unkindly doesn't help anyone feel better.

WHERE CAN IT COME FROM?

Are you making fun of others?

No one is perfect. You can look at anyone (including yourself) and find something to criticize or make fun of. Making fun of someone's weakness is very unkind.

Then try looking at the good things about others instead of their weaknesses. Tell your friends what you like about them. Do the same for your parents, brothers, and sisters. Help others feel good about themselves, and you'll feel better about yourself too.

Scripture:
Ephesians 4:29
Say what is good about others.

Are you a faultfinder?

You can make yourself feel important, strong, or smart by pointing out other people's faults and saying things that make them look less important, weak, or dumb. Does what you say make others feel bad?

Then try thinking about how the other person feels. Focus on others' strong points and do what you can to make them feel good about themselves. Encourage others any way you can.

Scripture:
1 Thessalonians 5:11
Build people up!

Are you a gossip?

Saying things about people behind their back is gossip! Do you want others to hear what you're saying? If they hear what you're saying, will they feel good or bad?

Then try saying nothing. Sometimes it's best to just be quiet. There's no reason to gossip. It just hurts someone and that can lead to anger and arguments. Just say no to gossip.

Scripture:
Proverbs 26:20
Silence brings peace.

CHECK OUT THIS SCRIPTURE. FIND IT IN YOUR BIBLE AND READ WHAT IT SAYS. IN ONE SENTENCE, WRITE WHAT YOU THINK IT SAYS.

1 Thessalonians 3:12-13 _____

_____

NOW, TRY THIS IDEA.

Draw a funny picture of yourself with love coming out everywhere. How will it come out of your ears? How about your fingernails? Then, every time you're tempted to gossip, remember your picture. Laugh at yourself and then ooze some love instead.

COMPLETE THE FOLLOWING

I chose not to gossip this week when I _____

_____ .

From now on, I'm going to avoid gossiping by _____

_____ .

Ephesians 4:29
   Say only what helps, each word a gift.

WHEN LIFE SEEMS REALLY HARD

Hey, there's no getting away from it—sometimes life is hard! Sometimes things aren't fair. Sometimes you have a lot of hard work to do. Sometimes things are just plain sad. Do you sometimes just want to crawl under a blanket and hide from everything?

WHERE CAN IT COME FROM?

Are you tired?

Do you have lots of homework? How about chores or worries? Any of these things can wear you out. Looking at lots of work can make you tired. Doing all that work can tire you out too.

Then try making a list. Write down what you need to do. Do one thing at a time. If you have one big thing to do, divide it into smaller parts. Cross things off when you get them done. Don't worry about getting everything done at once. Just do things one at a time.

Scripture:
Psalm 18:1-2
God will help you!

Are you sad?

You worked really hard on a school project and thought you did a great job, but your teacher didn't agree. Or maybe you have to move and leave all your friends. Life is hard when sad things happen.

Then try looking for the good. Think about the new friends you'll make or what you'll learn if you talk to your teacher. Look back over your life and see how things worked out in the past. Remember how God took care of you in other hard times. He'll help you now too.

Scripture:
Romans 8:38-39
Nothing can separate you from God.

Are you stuck?

Sometimes it can feel like you are just bumping into a brick wall over and over again. You keep trying to make friends or to understand math or to hit a baseball, but it just doesn't happen. These are hard things.

Then try not giving up. Keep on trying and trying and trying. You will succeed. Ask God to help you. He'll give you strength and courage to help you through this. What you learn by sticking with it you'll be able to use other times too! You can do it!

Scripture:
Matthew 7:7-8
Keep on asking.

CHECK OUT THIS SCRIPTURE. FIND IT IN YOUR BIBLE AND READ WHAT IT SAYS. IN ONE SENTENCE, WRITE WHAT YOU THINK IT SAYS.

Philippians 3:12-14 _____

_____

NOW, TRY THIS IDEA.

Start a stone collection. Every time you finish a hard thing, put a stone in a corner of your top drawer or in a bowl on your dresser. See how many stones you collect. See how many hard things you can do with God's help!

COMPLETE THE FOLLOWING

I learned that I can do hard things when _____

_____ .

From now on, I'm going to get hard things done by _____

_____ .

Lamentations 3:28
When life is heavy and hard to take, . . . wait for hope to appear.

WHEN I GET NERVOUS

You're walking into a new school or to the front of the class. You're getting ready for your first real baseball game. Your heart is pounding and your face feels hot and your stomach hurts. Why do these things happen?

WHERE CAN IT COME FROM?

Are you worried?

Do you spend a lot of time worrying about the worst that could happen? Do you focus on all the problems you might have or what might go wrong?

Then try giving it to God. God cares about everything that happens to you. Take time to talk with him about the things that make you nervous. Ask for his help and strength. Then think about how proud God is of you. God is cheering for you!

Scripture:
Philippians 4:6
Prayer brings
peace.

Are you afraid?

It's true that most everyone is afraid of something. Are you scared when you have to talk in front of your class? Are you afraid of high places? A little fear can help you stop and think. A lot of fear keeps you from thinking at all.

Then try trusting God. God promises that the Holy Spirit will help you through the hard things in life. If you have put your trust in him, there is no reason to be afraid. Do your best, knowing that God is with you and helping you.

Scripture:
Isaiah 41:10
Fear not! Help is on the way!

Are you imagining things?

Having an imagination is a good thing, but not when you let it run away with your thoughts. Imagining that terrible things will happen to you or that your friends will not understand can make things worse than they really are.

Then try imagining the good things that can happen. Memorize a Scripture verse and think about it over and over. You won't have time to imagine bad things if you fill your mind with good things!

Scripture:
Jeremiah 29:11
God has good plans for you!

CHECK OUT THIS SCRIPTURE. FIND IT IN YOUR BIBLE AND READ WHAT IT SAYS. IN ONE SENTENCE, WRITE WHAT YOU THINK IT SAYS.

Matthew 14:29-33 _____

_____

NOW, TRY THIS IDEA.

Think about how Peter must have felt stepping out of a boat onto a stormy sea! Find a piece of chalk and draw on the sidewalk a picture of when you're most nervous. Then take a pail of water and pour it on the picture and watch it wash away. That's what can happen to your fears if you let Jesus help you when you're nervous.

COMPLETE THE FOLLOWING

I learned that I don't get so nervous when I _____

_____ .

From now on, whenever I get nervous, I'm going to _____

_____ .

Philippians 4:6
Don't fret or worry. Instead of worrying, pray.

WHEN I GET STRESSED

Have you ever played with a toy that you have to wind up? It works until it winds down, unless you wind it up too tight. Then it doesn't work at all. When you're wound up tight, you're stressed. Everything is hard, and nothing works.

WHERE CAN IT COME FROM?

Are you in a hurry?

If you're in a hurry to get something done, you may not get it done right. If you're in a hurry to make friends or learn how to do something, you'll make lots of mistakes. Being in a hurry makes you feel like you have to keep going faster. That's very stressful.

Then try slowing down. You have plenty of time. God wants you to enjoy the life he gave you, not rush through it. If you slow down, you get things right the first time, and you'll actually get things done faster in the long run.

Scripture:
Psalm 118:24
Enjoy today!

Are you with wrong people?

Are your friends trying to tell you to do things that you know are wrong? Are they asking you to hide things you're doing or to tell lies? Are you talking to people at school or on the Internet you're not sure about? These things can make you feel like you're walking with a big weight on your back. Stress is like that.

Then try listening to your heart. If you feel worried or unsure about the friends you have or the people you're talking with, make a change. You know what's right and what's wrong. If you're doing something wrong, turn around and go the other way.

Scripture:
2 Thessalonians 3:6
Choose friends wisely.

Are the wrong things first?

What is most important in your life? Is it watching TV? Reading loads of good books? Being friends with everybody? Getting great grades? You may be trying to do too many things or trying to do things that just aren't as important as you think.

Then try looking at what's important. Take a good look at what you're spending your time doing and thinking about. God doesn't want you to be like anyone else. Ask him to show you what's most important for *you*.

Scripture:
Joshua 24:14-15
Choose what's most important.

CHECK OUT THIS SCRIPTURE. FIND IT IN YOUR BIBLE AND READ WHAT IT SAYS. IN ONE SENTENCE, WRITE WHAT YOU THINK IT SAYS.

Ecclesiastes 3:9-13 _____

_____

NOW, TRY THIS IDEA.

Take a minute to cool off. Take an ice cube out of the freezer and hold it in your hand (over the sink, of course). Watch how it melts in your hand. While it melts, think about the things that are causing you stress. Ask God to help you let them melt away by making good choices.

Choice **1**

Choice **2**

COMPLETE THE FOLLOWING

I learned that I don't get so stressed when I _____

_____ .

From now on, whenever I get stressed, I'm going to _____

_____ .

1 Peter 3:11
Snub evil and cultivate good; run after peace for all you're worth.

WHEN I CAN'T HAVE WHAT I WANT

"I want that!" How often do you say this? Do you have to get something every time you go somewhere? How often do you ask for something?

WHERE CAN IT COME FROM?

Are you jealous?

Jealousy is when you want what others have. When you see the stuff your friends have, are you happy for them or do you want it yourself?

Then try being happy with what you have. Look at all you have, and be happy with that. Be happy for others too, just like you want them to be happy for you.

Scripture:
1 Corinthians 13:4 Love doesn't get mad about others' success!

Are you selfish?

Do you focus on yourself most of the time? That's going to cause problems if you start to think that you are the most important person in the world and that the rest of the world owes you something.

Then try not focusing on yourself. You don't like it when others think of themselves all the time, so why is it okay for you? Try thinking of others first. You'll have lots more friends and lots more fun!

Scripture:
Philippians 2:3 Consider others first.

Are you unthankful?

If you always want what you can't have, you're probably not being thankful for what you do have. Thankfulness and an "I want that" attitude can't live in your heart at the same time.

Then try being thankful. Being thankful for what you already have will make you feel more satisfied. Take time to thank God for what you have. Thank others who give you things too. You'll be a lot happier.

Scripture:
Colossians 3:15 Peace rules through thankfulness.

CHECK OUT THIS SCRIPTURE. FIND IT IN YOUR BIBLE AND READ WHAT IT SAYS. IN ONE SENTENCE, WRITE WHAT YOU THINK IT SAYS.

1 Thessalonians 5:16-18 _____

_____

NOW, TRY THIS IDEA.

Go through all your stuff and make a pile of things you haven't used lately. Give those things to someone who will use them. Now, every time you ask for something new, give something else away.

COMPLETE THE FOLLOWING

Something I learned that I don't need is _____

_____ .

From now on, every time I see something I want, I'm going to _____

_____ .

1 Corinthians 13:4
Love doesn't want what it doesn't have.

WHEN I WATCH TOO MUCH TV

Are you a couch potato? Do you waste time with your attention glued to the TV? When you watch too much TV, other stuff doesn't get done. Often the undone stuff is more important than what you were watching.

WHERE CAN IT COME FROM?

Are you avoiding things?

Are there things you're supposed to do but don't want to do? Sometimes there are things you don't want to think about. Watching TV is easy because you don't have to think or do anything.

Then try facing the hard thing. What you're avoiding won't go away while you're watching TV. So just face it and get it over with. If there's a problem, ask for some help. The sooner you face it, the easier life will be.

Scripture:
Joshua 1:9
God goes with you!

Are you being lazy?

Do your mom and dad get mad at you because you don't do your chores or homework when you should? Do *you* get mad at you because you spend so much time watching TV when you could be getting those chores done or playing with friends?

Then try setting limits. It's okay to relax for a little while, but don't let it be all the time. Decide how much TV you're going to watch, and set a timer. Now make a list of at least three things you like to do. When the timer goes off, choose one of those things—and do it. Add to your fun list as often as you think of something else you can do.

Scripture:
Ephesians 5:15-16
Be careful how you live.

Are you bored?

What did you do yesterday? If your answer is "Nothing," you must be bored! But TV doesn't cure boredom. God created you with arms and legs so you would get up and be *you*, not sit and be a TV zombie.

Then try doing something! Use those arms and legs. If you don't have chores or homework, there are people who can use your help. Kids would love to have someone like you to play with. Maybe you know an elderly person who needs a helping hand. Give the special things only you can give. There's so much to do!

Scripture:
1 Peter 4:10
Do everything for God.

CHECK OUT THIS SCRIPTURE. FIND IT IN YOUR BIBLE AND READ WHAT IT SAYS. IN ONE SENTENCE, WRITE WHAT YOU THINK IT SAYS.

Proverbs 12:27 _____

_____

NOW, TRY THIS IDEA.

Think of something you can do for your brother, sister, mom, dad, or friend. It could be helping with chores, spending time with them, or making something for them. Do it as if you're doing it for God.

COMPLETE THE FOLLOWING

The best thing that happened when I turned off the TV was _____

_____ .

From now on, instead of watching too much TV, I'm going to _____

_____ .

Ephesians 5:11
Don't waste your time.

WHEN I'M AFRAID

Some things in life are scary. Just thinking about them can make your stomach hurt. Big storms, rushing water, and fast-moving cars are things to respect. New schools, dark places, and places you've never been before should be respected too. But respect and fear are two different things. Respect helps you think better, but fear can get in the way of thinking.

WHERE CAN IT COME FROM?

Do you think you'll fail?

Being afraid of failing can cause fear. When you think about the things you don't do well and remember all the times you've failed before, you're telling yourself you're not good. Does God agree with that?

Then try to focus on what you do well. God made you to be good at some things. Do those things mostly. When you have to tackle something hard, know that God will help you, and think about the times you've done things well. You don't have to be good at everything.

Scripture:
Psalm 27:1-2
With God's help you won't be afraid!

Is there danger?

Is someone making threats? Does a scary person bother you when you're not with others? These things can make you afraid, and you need to do something about it.

Then try taking action. Find a safe person and tell him or her about your fear. Let that person help you make wise choices about where you go and what you do. Ask God for wisdom too. He'll always be with you.

Scripture:
James 1:5
Ask for wisdom.

Are you in trouble?

Have you done something wrong? That's called sin, and sin causes all kinds of fear. There's fear of someone finding out what you did, fear of God, fear of the situation your choice put you in. There's only one way for these fears to go away.

Then try admitting what you did. If you admit your sin to God, he will help you. So, first go to God and ask for his forgiveness. He'll help you make things right. It might be hard at first, but not nearly as hard as being afraid all the time.

Scripture:
1 John 1:9
God helps when we tell on ourselves.

CHECK OUT THIS SCRIPTURE. FIND IT IN YOUR BIBLE AND READ WHAT IT SAYS. IN ONE SENTENCE, WRITE WHAT YOU THINK IT SAYS.

Psalm 91:1-6 _____

_____

NOW, TRY THIS IDEA.

Build a tent in your room out of blankets and pillows. Crawl inside and read Psalm 91:1-6. Think about how safe and cozy you feel in your tent. That's what it's like when you let God be your refuge, your safe place. Build your refuge anytime you want a safe, cozy place, and talk to God.

COMPLETE THE FOLLOWING

I stopped being afraid when I _____

_____ .

From now on, whenever I'm afraid, I'm going to _____

_____ .

Psalm 27:1
   With him on my side I'm fearless, afraid of no one and nothing.

WHEN I DON'T WANT TO OBEY

Everyone has rules to follow. Obeying is not something just kids have to think about. There are all kinds of reasons not to obey, and all of them get you into trouble. Learning to follow the rules is a sign of being grown-up.

WHERE CAN IT COME FROM?

Are you trying to be the boss?

Maybe you think you know what's best. Maybe you like to be in charge. You might be very smart and know lots of things. Sometimes this can be very good. But you need to be careful when you're trying to be the boss.

Then try following the rules. Before you can be a boss, you need to learn to follow rules. God will never give you big things to do if you won't obey rules.

Scripture:
Deuteronomy 7:9
It's good to obey God.

Are you being lazy?

Obeying can seem to be a lot of work. When you're a lazy person, you just don't want to put the effort into obeying.

Then stop being lazy! God makes it very clear that he doesn't like lazy people. Besides, if you don't do what you're asked now, you'll have to do it pretty soon anyway. You might as well just do it. Life is actually easier when you obey.

Scripture:
Deuteronomy 5:16
Things go well when you honor your parents.

Are you testing your limits?

Are you checking to see how much you can get away with? Are you trying to see how far you can push before you get in trouble? Why?

Then try thinking about what you're doing. Why do you feel you need to test your limits? Do you want more attention? Do you want more to eat? Wouldn't it be better to get attention for doing the right things or asking for what you need?

Scripture:
Galatians 6:4
Test your own actions.

CHECK OUT THIS SCRIPTURE. FIND IT IN YOUR BIBLE AND READ WHAT IT SAYS. IN ONE SENTENCE, WRITE WHAT YOU THINK IT SAYS.

Deuteronomy 5:32-33 _____

_____

NOW, TRY THIS IDEA.

Close your eyes and try walking around your house. Don't peek and be sure to go slowly. Think about how walking around blindly is like choosing not to obey. Are there some dangers? What is more difficult?

COMPLETE THE FOLLOWING

I obeyed when I _____

_____ .

From now on, I'm going to obey because _____

_____ .

Deuteronomy 5:16
    Respect your father and mother—GOD, your God, commands it! You'll have a long life.

WHEN I DON'T TAKE CARE OF MY THINGS

Do you leave your clothes piled on the floor . . . for days? Do you leave soccer balls and basketballs in the yard or your bicycle lying in the driveway? These are some examples of not taking care of your things.

WHERE CAN IT COME FROM?

Are you being wasteful?

If you think, "Oh, if my shoes get ruined, Mom will just buy me a new pair." That's wasteful.

Then try taking care of the things you have so they will last a long time. That's called being a good steward. Use wisely the things that God has allowed you to have.

Scripture:
Luke 16:10
Taking care of little things leads to big things.

Are you being lazy?

"I'm too tired to hang up my clothes." Do you think your mom is less tired? Will it be any less work to pick them up tomorrow? And won't it feel good to know you can keep your room clean?

Then try touching everything only once. Put things away instead of dropping them on the floor. If you drop it, you'll have to pick it up. That's touching it twice. It's less work in the long run to touch things only once.

Scripture:
2 Timothy 2:15
A good worker is not ashamed.

Are you not showing respect?

How would you feel if you gave something to a friend and then found it lying in the street? How do your family and friends feel about the things they've given you?

Then try showing respect. Show your family and friends that you value them by taking care of the things they've given you.

Scripture:
1 Peter 2:17
Show respect to everyone.

Proverbs 6:6-8 _____

_____

NOW, TRY THIS IDEA.

Go outside and watch some ants. Then come inside and get to work cleaning your room. Start in one corner and work your way around. Don't worry if you don't get it all done at once. Just keep doing some at a time. Find a place for everything. Be like an ant!

COMPLETE THE FOLLOWING

I took care of my things when I _____

_____ .

From now on, I'm going to care for my things because _____

_____ .

2 Timothy 2:15
   Concentrate on doing your best for God, work you won't be ashamed of.

WHEN I CHEAT

Did you know that cheating is just not smart? Besides the fact that cheating is wrong, cheaters don't win in the long run. Cheaters might get away with it for a little while, but it will always catch up with them. Cheating is not honest. God makes it very clear: being honest is very important.

WHERE CAN IT COME FROM?

Are you unsure of yourself?

Are you afraid of getting wrong answers? Are you unsure that you can do things the right way? Are you afraid that someone else will win the game you're playing?

Then try building your confidence. If you don't understand, ask for help. It's not so terrible to make mistakes either. Ask why and learn from it. Wise people have made lots of mistakes. Ask them and see.

Scripture:
Proverbs 3:25-26
Let your confidence come from God.

Are you proving something?

Are you trying to win friends by proving you can get away with cheating? What are you really proving by cheating?

Then try proving your honesty instead. The only friends you'll win by cheating are cheaters, and you don't want them as friends. Prove your honesty, and you'll find honest friends. And the only stuff that's really yours is stuff you got honestly.

Scripture:
Genesis 4:7
You'll be accepted if you do what is right.

Are you looking for attention?

Do you cheat and then brag about it? Do you think it's fun to get caught, because everyone notices you? Are you sure you want to be known for being a cheat?

Then try getting attention another way. No one will trust a cheater. You'll get lots more attention for being honest. You'll have more friends, because everyone likes someone they can trust. You'll have God's attention too. See if you get more attention for being honest.

Scripture:
1 John 1:6-7
Truth is right in the light.

CHECK OUT THIS SCRIPTURE. FIND IT IN YOUR BIBLE AND READ WHAT IT SAYS. IN ONE SENTENCE, WRITE WHAT YOU THINK IT SAYS.

Luke 6:43-45 _____

_____

NOW, TRY THIS IDEA.

Go outside and find a small branch that is lying on the ground. Stand it in a cup and then make some fruit out of scratch paper to hang on it. Think about the things you want to be known for, and write those things on each of the pieces of fruit. Use your tree as a reminder of the things you'll do instead of cheating.

COMPLETE THE FOLLOWING

I didn't cheat this week because _____

_____ .

From now on, I'm not going to cheat because _____

_____ .

Proverbs 16:11
GOD cares about honesty.

49

WHEN I GET PUNISHED

Being punished is not fun. But, believe it or not, there is actually a reason for it. You usually only get punished if you disobey or do the wrong thing. There are always consequences when you do something wrong, no matter how old you are. These things help you to be sorry and remind you not to do it again.

WHERE CAN IT COME FROM?

Did you disobey?

Did your mom ask you to do something and you didn't? Did your teacher tell you no, but you did it anyway? You know what's going to happen, don't you?

Then try learning from your mistakes. Take your punishment, and learn not to do whatever it was again. Face up to your mistake and take what you earned. Use your experience to get back on track. Discipline shows that someone cares about you. It shows they care enough to help you be a better person.

Scripture:
Proverbs 13:24
Loving discipline is best!

Were you in the wrong place?

Sometimes you're just in the wrong place at the wrong time. Maybe it's your friend who did the wrong thing, but you were there. Maybe your mom or dad was having a hard time, and you were demanding something.

Then try making wise choices. Choose your friends wisely and choose wisely where you go. Don't hang out with troublemakers. If your parents are having a hard time, try to give them some space. If it's really hard for them, encourage them to get some help.

Scripture:
Proverbs 12:1
Learn from being corrected.

Did you do something wrong?

Every one of us has this problem. We all mess up. It's called sin, and all of us are guilty. We seem to be born with it. Does this mean that sin is okay? Nope, it's still wrong. That's why you're being punished.

Then keep on trying. Do your very best not to sin. Most of the time you'll succeed. When you mess up, admit what you did. You'll earn lots of respect when you're honest about your mistakes.

Scripture:
Galatians 6:7
Grow what you sow.

CHECK OUT THIS SCRIPTURE. FIND IT IN YOUR BIBLE AND READ WHAT IT SAYS. IN ONE SENTENCE, WRITE WHAT YOU THINK IT SAYS.

Romans 7:15-19 _____

_____

NOW, TRY THIS IDEA.

Make a valentine for your mom or dad and give it to them. Tell them you love them. Talk with them about the punishment they have to give you. Ask how they feel about it.

COMPLETE THE FOLLOWING

The biggest thing I've learned from being punished is _____

_____ .

From now on, when I'm punished, I'll remember _____

_____ .

Proverbs 12:1
If you love learning, you love the discipline that goes with it.

WHEN I WANT WHAT OTHERS HAVE

Some pretty ugly words describe this feeling: jealousy, lust, envy, coveting. They all mean wanting what you don't have or what you see that someone else has. It can make you very unhappy. It can get you into trouble too.

WHERE CAN IT COME FROM?

Are you being unthankful?

When you think a lot about what you don't have, you're not going to be thankful for what you have. Do you have a place to live? Is it totally empty? Have you gone without food for more than a day? Have your arms and legs stopped working? Life's not all bad then.

Then try being thankful. Enjoy what you do have. When you look at all of your blessings, you'll be more satisfied—and happy.

Scripture:
1 Timothy 6:6-8
It's great to be satisfied!

Are you complaining?

Have you ever noticed that the more you complain, the unhappier you are? Complaining reminds you of what you are unhappy about. It can also make you unpleasant to be around.

Then try speaking well. Speaking about good things helps you focus on the positive things in your life. It makes you feel better and helps you be thankful for what you have.

Scripture:
Philippians 2:14
Speak good words and rejoice.

Are you being selfish?

Always focusing on yourself and thinking, "I'm the most important" can be a problem. It may mean you need more than everyone else. It may mean you don't think of anyone else. Is that what you want to be like?

Then try thinking about other people. Pay attention to their feelings and needs. Look at how many people have less than you do. See other people as important too.

Scripture:
Philippians 2:4
Look at others' needs.

CHECK OUT THIS SCRIPTURE. FIND IT IN YOUR BIBLE AND READ WHAT IT SAYS. IN ONE SENTENCE, WRITE WHAT YOU THINK IT SAYS.

Psalm 100 _____

_____

NOW, TRY THIS IDEA.

Plan a thank-you party. Ask your mom or dad if you can help fix her or his favorite meal. Invite the whole family. Spend the whole mealtime talking about all the things you're thankful for.

COMPLETE THE FOLLOWING

Today I'm most thankful for _____

_____ .

Every day I will give thanks for _____

_____ .

Philippians 2:4
Put yourself aside, and help others get ahead.

WHEN I HAVE TO BE FIRST

First across the finish line or first in line at school. First place in the art contest, the spelling bee, and the science fair. Do you need to be first in everything? Well, maybe not everything, but most things?

WHERE CAN IT COME FROM?

Are you being selfish?

Do you always want to be the winner, always be first, and always be the most important? How do you think others feel about that? Have you thought that maybe others would like to be first too?

Then try looking beyond yourself. Make an extra effort to think about other people and their feelings. Let others be first once in a while—you know how good it feels!

Scripture:
Matthew 7:12
Treat others like you want to be treated.

Are you full of pride?

Pride is thinking that what you do or think is more important or better than what others do or think. It puts other people down while lifting yourself up.

Then try putting others first. That's called being humble. Humble people don't always have to be first. They care about what others think and what they do. Humble people even encourage and praise others.

Scripture:
Proverbs 16:18
Pride trips us up.

Are you proving yourself?

When you don't feel good about yourself, then you try to be first to prove you're okay.

Then try looking at what God says about you. He created you. He gave you special gifts, strengths, and talents. He loves you so much he sent his only Son for you. He wants you to be his son or daughter too. You don't have to prove yourself if God thinks this much of you!

Scripture:
Ephesians 5:1
Keep your eyes on God.

CHECK OUT THIS SCRIPTURE. FIND IT IN YOUR BIBLE AND READ WHAT IT SAYS. IN ONE SENTENCE, WRITE WHAT YOU THINK IT SAYS.

Luke 9:46-48 _____

_____

NOW, TRY THIS IDEA.

Let others go first. Look for ways at home or at school to let others go first. See if you can do it five times today and tomorrow. Think about how it feels to let others be first on purpose.

COMPLETE THE FOLLOWING

When I let someone else go first this week, I felt _____

_____ .

I'm going to let others be first sometimes because _____

_____ .

Ephesians 5:1
   Watch what God does, and then you do it, like children who learn proper behavior from their parents. Mostly what God does is love you. Keep company with him and learn a life of love.

WHEN I WANT TO SKIP CHURCH

Would you rather sleep than go to church? Maybe you have a baseball game or your friend is having a birthday party. There are lots of reasons to skip church. Some of them sound pretty good. Our choices show what's most important to us.

WHERE CAN IT COME FROM?

Do you have to choose?

There are lots of other things that happen the same time as church and many of them seem important.

Then try deciding what's important to you. Where does God fit in your list compared to friends and sports? You'll be faced with these decisions all your life. It's not easy, now or when you're a grown-up.

Scripture:
Exodus 20:8-10
Keep the Sabbath holy.

Are you tired?

Do you stay up late doing other stuff? Are you so busy during the week that you are just plain tired? Do you want to sleep instead of go to church?

Then try figuring out how to get some sleep. When you're growing, sleep is important. Learning to get sleep at the right times is also important. If you're only tired when it's time to go to church, you might need to think about when you're getting your sleep.

Scripture:
Luke 10:42
Choose what's best.

Are you bored?

What is going on that's making you not want to get to church? Maybe your Sunday school class isn't exciting to you. Or maybe you don't have any friends at church.

Then try bringing a friend. Maybe you could think of what would help make your class more interesting and offer to do it. Maybe you need to sit in church with your mom or dad, or help with a younger class. Remember, too, that you're going to church to honor God.

Scripture:
Hebrews 10:24-25
Make the most of church.

CHECK OUT THIS SCRIPTURE. FIND IT IN YOUR BIBLE AND READ WHAT IT SAYS. IN ONE SENTENCE, WRITE WHAT YOU THINK IT SAYS.

Psalm 122:1 _____

_____

NOW, TRY THIS IDEA.

Do more than put your clothes on when you get ready for church this week. Look in the mirror and put on your attitude. Think about what God has done for you. What will you do to show God your thanks?

COMPLETE THE FOLLOWING

The one thing I can look forward to at church is _____

_____ .

Church is going to be a part of my life because _____

_____ .

Hebrews 10:24-25
> Let's see how inventive we can be in encouraging love and helping out, not avoiding worshiping together as some do but spurring each other on, especially as we see the big Day approaching.

WHEN I WORRY ABOUT HOW I LOOK

Do you look in the mirror a lot? How much time do you spend fixing your hair and choosing what to wear? Do you choose your friends based on how they look? It's important to take care of yourself, but sometimes you can go too far. Sometimes how you look becomes more important than who you are.

WHERE CAN IT COME FROM?

Are you being vain?

When your biggest thoughts are about how you look, it's called being vain. Looking in the mirror too much means you're looking more at your face than at your heart.

Then try looking at others. The most beautiful people in the world are those who care about others. Looking at others grows a good and beautiful person. Others will think you're more beautiful when you're looking at them and not yourself.

Scripture:
1 Peter 3:3-4
Beauty comes from gentleness.

Are you worried?

Are you worried that you're too fat or too thin? Are you worried that there's a problem with your body?

Then try asking someone who knows. Ask one of your parents or your doctor. Don't listen to those who don't really know, like some people on TV or kids at school. God made you to be a certain size and shape. If your mom and dad or doctor say you're fine, stop worrying and enjoy who God made you to be.

Scripture:
Psalm 139:14
God made you beautiful!

Are wrong things important?

Things that are important to us are called priorities. What you spend your time doing shows what your priorities are. What's most important to you? What are your priorities?

Then try looking at what's really important. God needs you to do much bigger things for him than look at yourself in a mirror. Look for the things God needs you to be doing!

Scripture:
Psalm 119:35-36
God will show you what's important.

CHECK OUT THIS SCRIPTURE. FIND IT IN YOUR BIBLE AND READ WHAT IT SAYS. IN ONE SENTENCE, WRITE WHAT YOU THINK IT SAYS.

1 Samuel 16:7 _____

_____

NOW, TRY THIS IDEA.

Make a self-portrait. Find a piece of paper as big as you are. You can even tape several pieces of newspaper together if you want. Lie on the paper and have someone trace your shape. Go over your outline with your favorite color of marker. Then write words on the inside of your shape that describe who you are. The only rule: You can't use any words that describe your outsides.

COMPLETE THE FOLLOWING

The best things about me are _____

_____.

I'm not going to worry so much about how I look because _____

_____.

Psalm 139:14
Body and soul, I am marvelously made!

59

WHEN I DON'T LISTEN TO OTHERS

Some people can't be told a thing. Do you refuse to listen when someone tries to help you? Do you think you know best all the time? Growing up, you get lots of advice. You're told how to do things a lot. You do know how to do some things, but when you think you know everything, that's a problem.

WHERE CAN IT COME FROM?

Are you being foolish?

The idea that you have all the answers and you know everything is foolish. You might be very smart, but no one knows *everything*—except God, of course.

Then try to listen to learn. Wise people know they can always learn something. Wise people want to keep learning. So listen with learning in mind. You'll keep getting smarter and wiser.

Scripture:
Proverbs 1:7
Listening makes you wise.

Are you ignoring wise help?

People who think they know everything show they really don't know anything. So don't ignore wise help. When people offer advice, it's because they want to help you.

Then try listening to advice. A person who wants to be wise pays close attention to wise help. It's okay to admit you don't know everything. In fact, really wise people will think you're very wise when you do.

Scripture:
Proverbs 13:1
Listen and be wise.

Are you being stubborn?

Refusing to listen to help is being stubborn. Stubborn people are like stubborn donkeys. They don't move, and no one thinks they know anything.

Then try taking a step. Take one step toward the person who's trying to help you. Smile and listen. See if there's something you can learn. See if others begin to listen to you too.

Scripture:
Job 36:10-12
Listening pays off.

CHECK OUT THIS SCRIPTURE. FIND IT IN YOUR BIBLE AND READ WHAT IT SAYS. IN ONE SENTENCE, WRITE WHAT YOU THINK IT SAYS.

Proverbs 4:5-7 _____

_____

NOW, TRY THIS IDEA.

Collect some wise advice. Ask some of the wise people you know (parents, grandparents, people at church) to tell you some of their wise advice. Write it down and make a little book. Share it with some of your friends or with the wise people who helped you put it together.

COMPLETE THE FOLLOWING

One thing I learned from listening is _____

_____ .

Listening will pay off because _____

_____ .

Proverbs 13:1
Intelligent children listen to their parents; foolish children do their own thing.

WHEN I CRY

Crying is okay sometimes. But some people cry about everything. That kind of person is not much fun to be around. Do you cry to get your way or to get attention? Do you cry to get others in trouble? There's good crying and not-so-good crying, and it's important to know the difference.

WHERE CAN IT COME FROM?

Are you sad?

Losing something or someone hurts and causes you to cry. If your dad or grandma or even your cat dies, it's very sad. Or maybe your parents got a divorce. You may cry a lot—and that's okay.

Then go ahead and cry. Even Jesus cried when he was sad. After you've cried for a while, ask Jesus to help you. It will take some time to start feeling happy again, but little by little the sadness will go away.

Scripture:
John 16:22-24
Jesus turns sadness into joy.

Did you mess up?

Everyone messes up once in a while. When you do, you might cry because you're embarrassed or sorry or frustrated. Failing is not fun, and you feel bad.

Then try making the best of it. Learn from your mistake. Think about what to do differently next time. You'll get another chance and, if you've thought about it—maybe even practiced it—you'll do much better.

Scripture:
Psalm 30:5
Joy comes in the morning!

Do you want your way?

Do you cry to get your way? Does it work? How do you think others feel about you when you act that way? Small children cry to get their way, but as you grow up, you'll learn more grown-up ways.

Then try explaining what you want. Grown-ups ask for what they want and explain why. Try being grown-up. Think about what you want and explain why it's important to you. See if others will listen to you more this way.

Scripture:
Luke 11:9-10
Ask for help.

CHECK OUT THIS SCRIPTURE. FIND IT IN YOUR BIBLE AND READ WHAT IT SAYS. IN ONE SENTENCE, WRITE WHAT YOU THINK IT SAYS.

Psalm 16:8-11 _____

_____

NOW, TRY THIS IDEA.

In Jerusalem there's a wall that is sometimes called the Wailing Wall, where people go to cry. Choose a place in your room and call it the Wailing Wall. Maybe it's your closet door or a corner of your room. Go there when you feel like crying. While you're there, talk with God about what's causing you to cry. Listen for his advice and help.

COMPLETE THE FOLLOWING

The difference between good crying and bad crying is _____

_____ .

When I feel like crying, I will remember _____

_____ .

Psalm 30:5
The nights of crying your eyes out give way to days of laughter.

WHEN I LOSE MY TEMPER

Do you know people who always lose their cool? Are you someone whose temper explodes at any little thing? How do you feel when that happens? How do those around you feel? Once in a while we all lose our temper. Most of the time, though, there's a better way to handle what's happening.

WHERE CAN IT COME FROM?

Are you looking for attention?

Do others give in and let you have your way when you have a temper tantrum? Do you want everyone to pay attention to you, so you make a big fuss?

Then try thinking about what you want, then ask for it. If you need time to think, go to another room, and then come back when you can ask calmly. You'll get lots more attention because others will want to be around you, and they'll want to listen to you.

Scripture:
Proverbs 14:16
Wisdom is cool.

Are there lots of little things?

Sometimes there are lots of little things bothering you. You had a little fight with your brother. You ran out of time for breakfast. You forgot your homework. Finally, one more thing goes wrong and you lose your temper.

Then try letting go of the little things. If you have a fight, work it out. Don't pretend things are okay if they aren't. Admit when you do something wrong; don't cover it up. This way, little things won't build up, and you won't explode.

Scripture:
Proverbs 15:18
Calm down.

Are you being mistreated?

Is someone hurting you? Is there someone making threats? These things can make you really mad because they're not fair.

Then try getting help. When others hurt you or scare you, you do get mad inside. Find a safe person and talk to him or her. Your temper will go away when you get some help.

Scripture:
Psalm 40:17
God can help!

CHECK OUT THIS SCRIPTURE. FIND IT IN YOUR BIBLE AND READ WHAT IT SAYS. IN ONE SENTENCE, WRITE WHAT YOU THINK IT SAYS.

Ephesians 4:26-27 _____

_____

NOW, TRY THIS IDEA.

Watch a sunset. Don't look at the sun; watch the clouds and the colors of the sky. Read Ephesians 4:26-27 again. If there's something making you mad, decide how to work on it before it gets dark.

COMPLETE THE FOLLOWING

I controlled my temper when _____

_____ .

Instead of losing my temper, I'm going to _____

_____ .

Proverbs 15:18
Hot tempers start fights; a calm, cool spirit keeps the peace.

WHEN I WANT MORE AND MORE

"Gotta have the biggest!" "Everyone else has it!" "I'll be the only one to have it!" "I want that!" Who says things like this? Could it be you? Well, you're not alone. We hear these things all the time, so it seems right to say them too.

WHERE CAN IT COME FROM?

Are you not satisfied?

How much more will you need to be happy? Just one more thing? Are you sure? When you have that, will you want something else? You may think that just this one thing will make you happy, but you'll most likely find something else you need too.

Then try being thankful for what you have. Count how many toys you have. Count your clothes. Then thank your parents for giving you what you have. You have a lot to be thankful for!

Scripture:
Hebrews 13:5
Be happy with what you have.

Are you greedy?

We all want some things, but TV tells you that you need more. Often friends tell you the same thing. Then you begin to believe it. Our wants get all mixed up with what we need.

Then try giving instead of getting. Share what you have and give to others. For every new thing you want, find at least one of your old things to give away. It can't be something that's worn out or broken either.

Scripture:
Ephesians 5:5
Greed gets you nowhere.

Are you impatient?

Do you want everything right now? If you can't wait for something, it's called being impatient. It's easy to see things we want and then expect that we should have them right away.

Then try waiting. See if you can wait until your birthday or Christmas to ask for more stuff. Make a list of the things you want and put them in the order you want them. Check your list next week and see if it's still the same.

Scripture:
James 5:7
Good things take time.

CHECK OUT THIS SCRIPTURE. FIND IT IN YOUR BIBLE AND READ WHAT IT SAYS. IN ONE SENTENCE, WRITE WHAT YOU THINK IT SAYS.

Philippians 4:11-12 _____

_____

NOW, TRY THIS IDEA.

Look through your room and get out the five most important things you have. Go and thank the person who gave each of them to you, or write a short thank-you note.

COMPLETE THE FOLLOWING

I found out I don't need so much because _____

_____ .

Every time I want something, I'm going to _____

_____ .

Hebrews 13:5
Don't be obsessed with getting more material things. Be relaxed with what you have.

WHEN I AM SICK

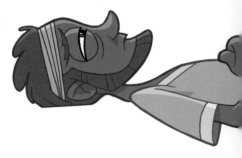

Everyone gets sick once in a while. Sometimes it's a cold or the flu. Sometimes it's a lot worse. Sometimes it comes because you haven't taken good care of yourself. Sometimes it just happens. No matter what, it's not fun.

WHERE CAN IT COME FROM?

Did you get a germ?

You feel awful. Your body is out of energy. You don't want to do anything.

Then try going to bed. Healing, by getting some rest, is what you need. Tell your parents and get into bed. Listen to advice from your parents or doctor. Ask God to help you feel better too.

Scripture:
Luke 4:40
Jesus heals the sick.

Are you not caring for yourself?

If you eat junk food, avoid getting exercise, and stay up too late, guess what can happen? Yep, you can get sick. Being sick is no fun.

Then try being smart about how you live. Take care of your body. It's the only one you have! God says our bodies are temples. A temple is a holy building. Keep yours well cared for!

Scripture:
1 Corinthians 6:19-20
Take care of the temple!

Are you really sick?

Maybe you have a serious illness. Your doctor will tell you if you have one. You may have to stay in bed for a long time and visit the doctor often. This doesn't happen very often.

Then try hanging in there. Make a list of all the things you can do in bed: read, draw, invent things, play card games, talk to people on the phone, pray. Use your list to remind yourself of things you can do while you're getting better.

Scripture:
James 1:2
Trials can be good.

CHECK OUT THIS SCRIPTURE. FIND IT IN YOUR BIBLE AND READ WHAT IT SAYS. IN ONE SENTENCE, WRITE WHAT YOU THINK IT SAYS.

Proverbs 15:30 _____

_____

NOW, TRY THIS IDEA.

Make a "feel better box." Find a shoe box and put stuff in it that you'll use only when you're sick, like paper and special markers, some Bible verses you've written on a paper, craft supplies, a joke book, and playing cards. Decorate the outside of the box and put it in a special place. If you know of someone who is sick, you might share your box with him or her.

COMPLETE THE FOLLOWING

When I get sick, I'll remember _____

_____ .

I can get through being sick if I _____

_____ .

James 1:2
Consider it a sheer gift, friends, when tests and challenges come at you from all sides.

WHEN I POUT AND WHINE

Do you stick out your bottom lip and pout when you don't get your way? Do you put on a sad face and whine to get attention? What you do when things don't happen the way you want tells a lot about how grown up you are.

WHERE CAN IT COME FROM?

Are you thinking only of yourself?

People who like whining don't care how they sound to other people. They don't care how they make other people feel either. When you whine, you sound bad, and you make others feel that way too.

Then try thinking about other people. Think about how you sound to them and how you make them feel. See if you can change the tone of your voice and find something nice to say. If you can't, it's best to just keep quiet.

Scripture:
Ecclesiastes 3:7
Know when to speak.

Are you expecting too much?

It would be nice if every decision were made so you'd be happy. But since you're not the only person in the world, this won't happen. Knowing how to deal with things when they're not what you had in mind is a good thing to learn.

Then try being real. Look at what happens to others. Do they always get their way? Are they whining or pouting? Probably not. Things just aren't always going to turn out the way you want. Sometimes they turn out better if you look for the good.

Scripture:
Haggai 1:5
Think about your actions.

Are you acting like a little child?

How often do you see adults pouting or hear them whine? Whining and pouting are things little children do. So, if you act that way, you're saying you aren't very grown up.

Then try taking a minute to think of a better way. If you take a minute to think, you'll be ale to explain how you feel or come up with a new idea. God will help you too, if you ask him.

Scripture:
1 Corinthians 13:11
Think like a grown-up.

CHECK OUT THIS SCRIPTURE. FIND IT IN YOUR BIBLE AND READ WHAT IT SAYS. IN ONE SENTENCE, WRITE WHAT YOU THINK IT SAYS.

Philippians 4:12-13 _____

_____

NOW, TRY THIS IDEA.

Make a list of things you might pout or whine about. Then, write a list of some better ways to handle those times.

_____   _____

_____   _____

_____   _____

_____

_____

_____

COMPLETE THE FOLLOWING

I'm giving up pouting and whining because _____

_____ .

Instead of pouting or whining, I'm going to _____

_____ .

Haggai 1:5
    Take a . . . hard look at your life. Think it over.

WHEN I DON'T WANT TO HELP OTHERS

Everyone needs help sometimes. Many times others need help when you're busy or you want to do something else. Usually, helping someone else means you'll have to give up doing something you want to do.

WHERE CAN IT COME FROM?

Do you think you can't?

Sometimes the job looks too big or you feel you're too young. Sometimes you just don't see how you can help.

Then try getting others to help too. No job is too big if there's enough help. Start asking others and see who will join you. If it's something God wants you to help with, he will show you a way.

Scripture:
Ecclesiastes 4:9-10
Two are better than one.

Are you too busy?

Everyone has lots to do. You're no exception. You have chores and schoolwork and friends and lessons and things you like to do. So does most everyone. You may wonder how you can get everything done.

Then try trusting God. Ask God to show you how to help and still get everything done. You'll be surprised how much time you have if you include God and helping others in your plan.

Scripture:
Proverbs 3:27
Don't wait to help.

Are you being lazy?

Lazy people ignore times to help others because they don't want to do work. Do you think it'll be too hard or too tiring? Do you just want to sit and read or watch TV?

Then try helping, you might like it. Helping others makes you feel better about yourself. You'll find energy you didn't know you had, and you'll have more fun than you think.

Scripture:
Luke 10:30-37
Love your neighbors, whoever they are.

CHECK OUT THIS SCRIPTURE. FIND IT IN YOUR BIBLE AND READ WHAT IT SAYS. IN ONE SENTENCE, WRITE WHAT YOU THINK IT SAYS.

Matthew 15:34-40 _____

_____

NOW, TRY THIS IDEA.

Look for one person who needs help. Help that person as if he or she were Jesus. Then thank Jesus for giving you the opportunity to help someone.

COMPLETE THE FOLLOWING

When I help others I feel _____

_____ .

I'm going to help others because _____

_____ .

Proverbs 3:27
Never walk away from someone who deserves help; your hand is *God's* hand for that person.

73

WHEN I'M IMPATIENT

It's so hard to wait, isn't it? Waiting with a bad attitude is being impatient. There are lots of different reasons for being impatient, and they all may sound like good ones. The weird thing is that being impatient won't change any of the things that cause it. So why be impatient?

WHERE CAN IT COME FROM?

Are you worried?

Are you worried about being first or having the most or not having enough? Are you worried you'll miss something? Will worry change any of these things?

Then try relaxing. Remember that God is in control of your life. He knows what you need and when you need it. He promises to be with you all the time. Besides, worrying won't change anything.

Scripture:
Psalm 27:14
Wait for God.

Are you in a hurry?

There is an old saying "Haste makes waste." And it is very true. Being in a hurry can cause you to lose a friend, miss learning something important, or have to do something over again.

Then try slowing down. Let things happen as they're supposed to. Take your time and treat people nicely. Do things the right way.

Scripture:
Proverbs 19:2
Haste makes waste.

Are you being foolish?

A foolish person rushes into things like a bull in a china shop. Do you know what happens when a bull runs in a china shop? Lots of things get broken.

Then try taking the time to understand what's happening. Look around and see what you can learn—or do—while you're waiting. God can show you many things if you take the time to look. Others will think you're very wise too!

Scripture:
Proverbs 14:29
Patience brings understanding.

CHECK OUT THIS SCRIPTURE. FIND IT IN YOUR BIBLE AND READ WHAT IT SAYS. IN ONE SENTENCE, WRITE WHAT YOU THINK IT SAYS.

Psalm 37:1-9 _____

_____

NOW, TRY THIS IDEA.

Find a cozy spot and enjoy it for ten minutes. Time yourself. See if you can sit really still for a whole ten minutes. While you're waiting, see what you can notice that you've not noticed before. What do you hear, what do you see, what do you smell? Think about how this is like waiting for other things you want.

COMPLETE THE FOLLOWING

I don't need to be impatient because _____

_____ .

When I'm feeling impatient, I'm going to _____

_____ .

Psalm 27:14
Stay with GOD! Take heart. Don't quit.

WHEN I TAKE SOMETHING THAT'S NOT MINE

What do you think when you take something that belongs to someone else? Do you think others won't notice or care? Do you think it should belong to you? Do you think it's okay to take what belongs to someone else? Let's think about this.

WHERE CAN IT COME FROM?

Are you stealing?

You can call it other things like borrowing or trying it out, but taking something that belongs to someone else is stealing. If you didn't buy it or have it given to you, it's not yours.

Then try being honest. If you want something, buy it or ask to borrow it. Don't take what isn't yours without asking.

Scripture:
Deuteronomy 5:19
No stealing.

Are you being greedy?

Greed is when money and things are more important to you than people and their feelings. Greed causes you to think only about yourself and not about others.

Then try putting yourself in others' shoes. Think about how they feel when something of theirs is missing. Think about what they'll think of you when they find out you took it.

Scripture:
Romans 13:9-10
Love doesn't steal.

Are you testing your limits?

Are you showing off? Are you trying to see what you can get away with? Is taking other people's things a game you're playing?

Then try thinking about what you're doing. Is it right to do these things? Talk with someone you trust about what you're doing and ask him or her to help you. God has big plans for your life, and he'll help you do it—without your taking what isn't yours.

Scripture:
Exodus 20:15
Just don't do it.

CHECK OUT THIS SCRIPTURE. FIND IT IN YOUR BIBLE AND READ WHAT IT SAYS. IN ONE SENTENCE, WRITE WHAT YOU THINK IT SAYS.

Luke 19:1-10 _____

_____

NOW, TRY THIS IDEA.

Go on a hunt. Take Jesus with you. Find everything that isn't yours and return it. It might be just one or two things, or it might be a whole box full. Ask Jesus to help you know what to say when you return the things you find.

COMPLETE THE FOLLOWING

I'm not going to take things that aren't mine because _____

_____ .

From now on, instead of taking, I'm going to _____

_____ .

Romans 13:9
> The law code— . . . don't take what isn't yours, don't always be wanting what you don't have, and any other "don't" you can think of—finally adds up to this: Love other people as well as you do yourself.

WHEN I DOUBT GOD

God never changes. He's always working, taking care of us, and guiding us. We know this is true, but sometimes we wonder. Sometimes God seems far away. Sometimes other people say things that make us wonder. God understands, even though we don't.

WHERE CAN IT COME FROM?

Are you feeling alone?

Do you feel like no one is your friend, not even God? Do you feel so alone that you're not sure God is there?

Then try proving yourself wrong. Ask three adults you trust if you're alone and have no friends, not even God. Watch a sunset or a sunrise. Think about how your brain thinks or your eyes see. Could anyone but God have created these things? Keep talking to God too. Sometimes God waits for what seems like a long time.

Scripture:
Psalm 94:9
He who created ears hears you!

Are you looking for God?

Are you seeing bad things happening? Did you see death or a storm that caused lots of ruin? It's easy to wonder where God is when you see bad things happen. Lots of people, even God's people, wonder.

Then try talking to God. He doesn't mind when you ask him these questions. The whole book of Habakkuk in the Bible is about Habakkuk asking God why he let bad things happen. You might want to read it to see what Habakkuk found out.

Scripture:
Habakkuk 3:17-18
Rejoice, no matter what.

Are you not hearing answers?

Do you keep asking God for something and you still haven't heard an answer? Are you wondering if God will ever answer?

Then try remembering. Think about the times when God did answer your prayers. Look in your Bible too. There are lots of examples of times when people waited a long time for God to answer their prayers. You might read about Samuel or Job, for starters.

Scripture:
Psalm 118:5-6
God does answer.

CHECK OUT THIS SCRIPTURE. FIND IT IN YOUR BIBLE AND READ WHAT IT SAYS. IN ONE SENTENCE, WRITE WHAT YOU THINK IT SAYS.

Genesis 12:6-7 _____

_____

NOW, TRY THIS IDEA.

In Old Testament times, people would build an altar to remind themselves of something God did. Collect some stones. Write one thing God has done for you on each of the stones. Then stack them up into your own altar of remembering. Put it where it'll remind you of all the things God has done for you.

COMPLETE THE FOLLOWING

When I doubt God, it's usually because _____
_____ .

From now on, when I doubt God, I'm going to _____
_____ .

Psalm 94:9
Do you think Ear-Maker doesn't hear, Eye-Shaper doesn't see?

WHEN MY WORDS AND ACTIONS DON'T MATCH

Do you tell everyone to be honest and then tell a lie? Do you tell others to love everyone and then mistreat a kid at school? Do you tell your friends to respect you and then talk about them when they're not around? What you do can speak louder than what you say.

WHERE CAN IT COME FROM?

Are you trying your best?

Paul, one of the greatest disciples, had a problem with his actions not matching his words. He tried his best and still messed up. We all do.

Then try telling on yourself. Tell God when you mess up, and ask him to help you do better. Don't give up. God understands, and he's always ready to help you.

Scripture:
Psalm 32:5
God forgives.

Are others getting you into trouble?

Are there some people who get you to do things you know you shouldn't? Are you different when you're with them?

Then try staying away. You already knew this, didn't you? Stay away from people who get you into trouble or suggest you do wrong things. Spend your time with people who encourage you to do what's right. It might be hard, but you can do it.

Scripture:
Ephesians 4:14-15
Be influenced by Jesus.

Are you ignoring God?

If you know what's right and you're just not doing it, then you're ignoring God. Are you angry with God? Are you angry with your parents? Doing what you know is wrong won't help.

Then try being honest with yourself. Talk to someone you trust and ask him or her to help you. If you're mad at God, tell him. He can handle it—and he'll help you through it.

Scripture:
Luke 15:7
God is happy when you return to him!

CHECK OUT THIS SCRIPTURE. FIND IT IN YOUR BIBLE AND READ WHAT IT SAYS. IN ONE SENTENCE, WRITE WHAT YOU THINK IT SAYS.

Galatians 6:7-10 _____

_____

NOW, TRY THIS IDEA.

Plant some seeds and watch them grow. You'll have to wait a number of days for them to sprout, so be patient. While you're waiting, think about a different kind of seed that you plant: The things you do and say are seeds. Good words grow good friends and so do good actions.

COMPLETE THE FOLLOWING

I feel better now because _____

_____ .

I can help my words and actions match by _____

_____ .

Luke 15:7

Count on it—there's more joy in heaven over one sinner's rescued life than over ninety-nine good people in no need of rescue.

WHEN I MUST HAVE EVERYTHING MY WAY

Do you always know the best way to do things? Do you always have to be the boss? There's nothing wrong with being smart and having good ideas. But no one will want to hear your ideas or do things your way if it's always about you.

WHERE CAN IT COME FROM?

Are you trying to help?

If you want to take charge to be helpful, God may have made you to be a leader. As you're growing up, you'll need to learn how to do it wisely. The best leaders learn how to work with others, not tell them what to do.

Then try listening to others. If you listen first, you'll get even more good ideas. And others will think you're wise and be willing to listen to you. Ask God to help you use your leadership gift wisely.

Scripture:
1 Kings 3:9-13
God loves it when you listen.

Do you have to be right?

We all want to be right. When it comes to how to do some things, there may be more than one good way to do it. Often there's not a right way and a wrong way; there are just different ways.

Then try listening and learning. Others will respect you if you listen to them and ask questions. They'll listen to you more too. Who knows, maybe you'll find another great way to do what you want to do.

Scripture:
Psalm 133:1
Getting along is good.

Are you being narrow-minded?

It's easy to know how *you* want to do something, because you're you. However, there's usually more than one way to do something. If there were only one way, everyone would be thinking the same way you are.

Then try looking at things differently. Look at how others want to do things and talk about their ideas. The best way may be their way or your way or both ways together.

Scripture:
Proverbs 3:7-8
Let God know it all, not you.

CHECK OUT THIS SCRIPTURE. FIND IT IN YOUR BIBLE AND READ WHAT IT SAYS. IN ONE SENTENCE, WRITE WHAT YOU THINK IT SAYS.

2 Kings 5:1-15 _____

_____

NOW, TRY THIS IDEA.

Take a shower or bath—backward. Think about the order you usually do things, and then do it backward. If you wash your feet last, do them first. How does doing something a different way help you to think differently?

COMPLETE THE FOLLOWING

By doing something another way I can learn _____

_____ .

Before insisting on doing it my way, I'm going to _____

_____ .

Proverbs 3:7
Don't assume that you know it all. Run to GOD! Run from evil!

WHEN I MISTREAT OTHERS

Do you say unkind things to your parents? Do you hit your little brother or boss your little sister? Do you give some people mean looks or just ignore them? Maybe they deserve it; maybe they don't. What do you think you're saying about yourself when you do these things?

WHERE CAN IT COME FROM?

Are you proving something?

Are you trying to prove that you're the boss? Are you trying to show your strength or what you know? Are you sure you're proving it the right way?

Then try listening to what God says. He says you're great. He says you don't have to prove anything. God says he loves you.

Scripture:
Psalm 149:4
God delights in you.

Are you getting even?

When you try to get even with people who have hurt you, it often leads to bigger problems. They'll just get back at you, and things will keep getting worse.

Then try leaving it to God. If someone really deserves to be punished, let God take care of it. God knows best what to do.

Scripture:
Deuteronomy 32:35
Let God take care of it.

Are you being hurt?

Has someone hurt your feelings or made you look bad? Is there someone picking on you? Are you tired of being left out? These things can make you want to hurt others.

Then try making some changes. Find different friends who treat you nicely. Don't go where the bullies are. Ask for some help in dealing with them. Then look to God to see what he says about you.

Scripture:
Romans 8:35-37
Nothing can separate you from God.

CHECK OUT THIS SCRIPTURE. FIND IT IN YOUR BIBLE AND READ WHAT IT SAYS. IN ONE SENTENCE, WRITE WHAT YOU THINK IT SAYS.

1 Corinthians 13:4-7 _____

_____

NOW, TRY THIS IDEA.

Go outside and find at least ten stones. Put them in a pile next to a small box or bag. Put one in the box or bag every time you do something kind or good for someone instead of mistreating that person. See if you can use all your stones this week. Next week, try it again!

COMPLETE THE FOLLOWING

I shouldn't mistreat others because _____

_____ .

Instead of mistreating others, I'm going to _____

_____ .

Romans 8:36-37
Do you think anyone is going to be able to drive a wedge between us and Christ's love for us? There is no way! Not trouble, not hard times, not hatred, not hunger, not homelessness, not bullying threats, not backstabbing, not even the worst sins listed in Scripture.

WHEN I MAKE EXCUSES

When you mess up, do you blame someone else or the weather or your dog? When things don't turn out right, is it everyone's fault but yours? When you don't get something done, do you have at least ten good reasons why?

WHERE CAN IT COME FROM?

Are you avoiding responsibility?

If you did something wrong and you're blaming others, you're avoiding responsibility. It may seem like the easy way out, but it's not. It's a lot of work to remember your excuses. Sooner or later, you'll be found out.

Then try telling on yourself. If you mess up, fess up. If there's punishment, take it. You'll earn respect from others and remember not to do that again.

Scripture:
Proverbs 21:2-3
God knows our hearts.

Are you denying the truth?

Are you blaming others because you're afraid of what will happen? Saying you didn't do something doesn't change the truth.

Then try telling the truth. This takes courage! Ask God to help you. Being honest pays off because others will know they can trust you.

Scripture:
Ephesians 4:15
Speaking the truth helps you grow.

Are you being lazy?

Do you make excuses because you don't want to do something like homework or cleaning your room or taking out the trash? Making an excuse doesn't make the work go away.

Then try just doing it. You might as well do what you're supposed to now, so you can have fun later. Having the fun now isn't really as much fun, because you're still thinking about the work you have to do.

Scripture:
Proverbs 15:20
You can make your parents proud!

CHECK OUT THIS SCRIPTURE. FIND IT IN YOUR BIBLE AND READ WHAT IT SAYS. IN ONE SENTENCE, WRITE WHAT YOU THINK IT SAYS.

Psalm 15:1-5 _____

_____

NOW, TRY THIS IDEA.

Ask your parents or grandparents about a time when they made a mistake and then covered it up with an excuse. What did they learn? Ask them to help you make a list of ten reasons not to make excuses.

COMPLETE THE FOLLOWING

Excuses don't help because _____

_____ .

No more excuses for me! Instead, I'm going to _____

_____ .

Proverbs 21:3
Clean living before God and justice with our neighbors mean far more to GOD than religious performance.

WHEN I WANT TO DO THE WRONG THING

Maybe you want to say bad words or watch things on TV you were told not to. Maybe you want to try something your friends are trying, but you're not sure about it. There are lots of choices you make every day. Many of them are choosing between right and wrong. Some are easy choices; some are not.

WHERE CAN IT COME FROM?

Are you checking things out?

Are you curious about things? Are you thinking you'll just check to see if what your parents told you is true? Are you wondering about something you haven't learned about yet?

Then try checking in first. Tell your mom and dad what you're thinking about. Ask them your questions. Don't do things you're not sure about without checking with your parents. They'll help you think things through.

Scripture:
Colossians 4:5-6
Use your head.

Are you listening to the wrong people?

Are you letting friends or older kids tell you what to think and do? Are you sure they're smarter than your parents? Are you sure they're the right people to listen to?

Then try listening to God first. If you wouldn't want God standing right there next to you while you're doing something, chances are you shouldn't be doing it.

Scripture:
Romans 16:17-19
Don't get comfy with evil!

Are you proving someone wrong?

Do you think you can prove that something is okay when your parents tell you it's wrong? Do you think you're smarter than your teachers?

Then try looking in the Bible. It talks a lot about where wisdom comes from. It comes from honoring your parents and listening to other wise people.

Scripture:
Exodus 20:12
Respect your dad and mom.

CHECK OUT THIS SCRIPTURE. FIND IT IN YOUR BIBLE AND READ WHAT IT SAYS. IN ONE SENTENCE, WRITE WHAT YOU THINK IT SAYS.

Genesis 45:24 _____

_____

NOW, TRY THIS IDEA.

Go for a walk. While you're walking, think about what it's like to walk with God. Think about taking God with you wherever you go.

COMPLETE THE FOLLOWING

The best way to decide if something is wrong is to _____

_____ .

When I'm thinking about something that might be wrong, I'm going to _____

_____ .

Colossians 4:5-6
Use your heads as you live and work among outsiders. Don't miss a trick. Make the most of every opportunity. Be gracious in your speech. The goal is to bring out the best in others in a conversation, not put them down, not cut them out.

WHEN I DON'T WANT TO GO TO SCHOOL

Sometimes it seems like school goes on and on, doesn't it? Do you get tired of school or feel like you've learned enough? Do you like the kids and your teacher? Figuring out why you don't want to go may help you.

WHERE CAN IT COME FROM?

Are you tired?

Are you still tired when you get up in the morning? Did you stay up too late reading or watching TV or playing video games?

Then try getting more sleep. School is so important. Look for ways to go to bed earlier on school nights. Save staying up late for Fridays.

Scripture:
Proverbs 18:15
Knowledge rules!

Are you afraid?

Are you afraid of doing poorly? Does the work feel too hard? Are you afraid of some of the kids there? Being afraid takes the fun out of school, for sure.

Then try asking for help. If you don't understand things, talk with your teacher or your parents, and tell them what's hard for you. That goes for scary kids too. There are lots of people who can help you.

Scripture:
Psalm 121:1-3
God is always with you.

Are you bored?

Do you already know a lot of what your teacher is telling you? Would you like school more if it gave you more to think about?

Then try looking for ways to use your brain. Respectfully talk to your teacher. Find out if there are extra things you can be doing that will get your brain going and help you be excited about school.

Scripture:
Proverbs 8:10-11
Go for the gold!

CHECK OUT THIS SCRIPTURE. FIND IT IN YOUR BIBLE AND READ WHAT IT SAYS. IN ONE SENTENCE, WRITE WHAT YOU THINK IT SAYS.

Proverbs 24:3-5 _____

_____

NOW, TRY THIS IDEA.

Build a little house. You can use paper, craft sticks, or a toy building set. Think about what you want in your house. Is it junk or cool stuff? How do you get smart enough to know about houses and what to put in them?

COMPLETE THE FOLLOWING

I'm going to value school because _____

_____.

The next time I don't want to go to school, I'm going to _____

_____.

Proverbs 18:15
Wise men and women are always learning, always listening for fresh insights.

WHEN MY FAMILY IS HAVING PROBLEMS

Did you know that every family has problems? Since no one is perfect, there will always be problems when more than one person lives in one place. Sometimes the problems are little; sometimes they're big. Working through them is part of life. Think of safe adults you can talk to about your problems, like a grandparent or teacher.

WHERE CAN IT COME FROM?

Are your parents fighting?

Fights happen because no two people are alike or will see things the same way. So this will happen with your parents. If they're fighting a lot, you might get very worried. You care for them and you don't know what will happen.

Then try giving them some space. Know that they love you and that their fights are not your fault. They need to work out their differences, and it's best to let them do it between themselves. Pray for them and look for ways to show them you love them.

Scripture:
Deuteronomy 5:16
Respect your father and mother.

Is someone really sick?

Maybe it's your mom or your grandfather or your aunt. When someone is very sick, it means that one or both of your parents will be very busy. This kind of stress causes everyone to be worried. It might be that money will be a little short because taking care of a sick person is very expensive.

Then try helping with what you can. Look around and see what you can do to help. Maybe it's with cleaning the house or watching a little brother or sister. Know that your family would like to be giving you more attention, and they will as soon as they can. When their temper is short, it's not because of what you've done; it's just their stress.

Scripture:
Romans 14:17
God is pleased when we help others.

Is someone in trouble?

Has someone in your family done something wrong? It could be that your older brother made a mistake at school or maybe your dad made a poor choice at work. You didn't cause the problem, but since you're part of the family, it still affects you.

Then try waiting. It's hard to be the one just watching all that is going on. You might want some attention too. Set an example by doing what's right. Know that you'll get the best attention when you're doing the right things.

Scripture:
James 1:2-4
Trials can bring out your best.

CHECK OUT THIS SCRIPTURE. FIND IT IN YOUR BIBLE AND READ WHAT IT SAYS. IN ONE SENTENCE, WRITE WHAT YOU THINK IT SAYS.

Matthew 5:14-16 _____

_____

NOW, TRY THIS IDEA.

Find a flashlight and go in a room where you can make it very dark. Turn on your flashlight and turn off the lights. Think about how you can be a light when times feel dark.

COMPLETE THE FOLLOWING

I can be a light to my family by _____

_____ .

When my family has a problem, I know I can _____

_____ .

James 1:2
You know that under pressure, your faith-life is forced into the open and shows its true colors.

WHEN I DON'T KNOW WHAT TO DO

There are lots of times when you just won't know what to do. Maybe you have to choose between helping a friend and getting your own work done. Maybe your friend has told you a secret and you think you need to tell your parents. Maybe you're worried about bad things that are happening in the world.

WHERE CAN IT COME FROM?

Do you have hard choices?

Maybe you've been told to do something that you think is wrong. Maybe you have to choose between helping at church and helping your grandmother. There are lots of times when you'll have to make hard choices.

Then try asking for some wise help. Go to the wisest person you know and ask him or her to help you think about your choices. You will face hard choices many times in life. It's good to learn to think about how to make good choices. God will help you too, if you ask him.

Scripture:
Proverbs 20:18
Seek wise advice.

Do you need help?

Maybe your friend is in trouble, but he or she doesn't want you to tell anyone. Maybe you want to help, but don't know how. Maybe you've been threatened and told not to let anyone know.

Then try finding a safe person to talk to. Any time someone tells you not to tell anyone, you should see a problem. Hiding things is seldom a good idea. So find a safe person and tell him or her about what's happening. Get that person's advice and let him or her help you.

Scripture:
Proverbs 18:24
A real friend sticks by you.

Are you worried?

Maybe you've seen or heard something and you're scared. Maybe you learned about something at school or on the news that's really bad, and you're worried it could happen to you.

Then try talking about it. Talk with your parents about how you're feeling. Ask them to help you sort things out. Talk with God too. He may not change things, but he will be with you and help you.

Scripture:
Proverbs 12:5
Good people make good plans.

CHECK OUT THIS SCRIPTURE. FIND IT IN YOUR BIBLE AND READ WHAT IT SAYS. IN ONE SENTENCE, WRITE WHAT YOU THINK IT SAYS.

Daniel 12:3 _____

_____

NOW, TRY THIS IDEA.

Paint a picture of yourself wearing shiny clothes or armor. Around your picture, put the names of people who will help you be wise and shine.

COMPLETE THE FOLLOWING

I figured out what to do by _____

_____ .

Next time I don't know what to do, I'll feel better because _____

_____ .

Proverbs 20:18
Form your purpose by asking for counsel, then carry it out using all the help you can get.

WHEN I'M _____

Write out your problem here: _____

_____

_____

_____

WHERE CAN IT COME FROM?

Are you _____

_____

_____

_____

_____

_____

_____

_____

Scripture

_____

_____

Are you _____

_____

_____

_____

_____

_____

_____

_____

Scripture

_____

_____

Are you _____

_____

_____

_____

_____

_____

_____

_____

Scripture

_____

_____

WRITE OUT A SCRIPTURE FROM YOUR BIBLE THAT HELPS YOU. THEN, IN ONE SENTENCE, WRITE WHAT YOU THINK IT SAYS.

Scripture _____

_____

_____

WHAT IT SAYS TO ME _____

_____

_____

WRITE AN IDEA OF SOMETHING YOU CAN DO TO APPLY THIS LESSON _____

_____

_____

COMPLETE THE FOLLOWING

I don't need to be _____ because _____

_____ .

When I am feeling _____ , I'm going to _____

_____ .

Find one more verse in your Bible that can help you with your problem and write it here: _____

_____

WHEN I'M _____

Write out your problem here: _____
_____
_____
_____

WHERE CAN IT COME FROM?

Are you _____
_____
_____
_____
_____
_____
_____
_____

Scripture
_____
_____
_____

Are you _____
_____
_____
_____
_____
_____
_____
_____

Scripture
_____
_____
_____

Are you _____
_____
_____
_____
_____
_____
_____
_____

Scripture
_____
_____
_____

WRITE OUT A SCRIPTURE FROM YOUR BIBLE THAT HELPS YOU. THEN, IN ONE SENTENCE, WRITE WHAT YOU THINK IT SAYS.

Scripture _____

_____

_____

WHAT IT SAYS TO ME _____

_____

_____

WRITE AN IDEA OF SOMETHING YOU CAN DO TO APPLY THIS LESSON _____

_____

_____

COMPLETE THE FOLLOWING

I don't need to be _____ because _____

_____ .

When I am feeling _____ , I'm going to _____

_____ .

Find one more verse in your Bible that can help you with your problem and write it here: _____

BIBLE DICTIONARY

INTRODUCTION TO THE DICTIONARY

A dictionary is a list of words and what they mean. This dictionary does way more than that. We tell you what the word means at the beginning. Then we take a look at six different places where you'll find that word in the Bible. Then we give you something to try to help you understand how that word works in your life. You'll really understand that word then!

We put all the words in order, so you can find them a little easier. (We couldn't figure out a good way to do that in the concordance section. Sorry!) So, look through the list of words, and when you find one you're curious about, go to that page and see what you can learn.

You might want to start with the last word in this dictionary, *wisdom*, because that's what you'll be collecting. The more you learn, the more full of wisdom you'll be. This world needs more wise people who know what God says. When you grow up, maybe you can write a book to help others or use your wisdom to take care of people or to teach them or to be a leader. You can also add your own words to this dictionary by using the blank pages at the end of this section.

BIBLE

WHAT THE BIBLE IS ALL ABOUT

The Bible is God's Word for us. In it you can find true stories about things that happened a long time ago. You can find wisdom and good advice. You can find out all about Jesus. When you read your Bible, you'll learn a lot about God and yourself.

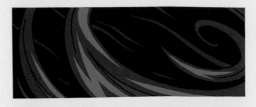

Look at what the Bible has to say about it:

Joshua 1:8   Think about what's in the Bible all the time.

Psalm 119:9-11   Put the words of the Bible in your heart.

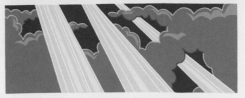

Psalm 119:72   The Bible is better than money.

Matthew 22:29   Knowing the Bible means knowing God's power.

Acts 18:28   The Bible proves Jesus is the Christ.

2 Timothy 3:16-17   The Bible trains and prepares you.

Open your Bible to James or Luke or Genesis. You can choose which one. Read just a few of the verses and think about what they're saying to you. Mark the page, then come back and read a few more verses tomorrow. Try reading a few verses every day and see what you've learned by the end of the week. Think of how you can make time to read even one or two verses from your Bible every day.

CHARACTER

WHAT CHARACTER IS ALL ABOUT

Character is all of your actions added together. Do people say, "She's always honest" or "He's always helping others"? What people say about how you usually act is your character.

Look at what the Bible has to say about character:

Genesis 4:7   Do what's right.

Psalm 143:10   Teach me to do what's right.

Zephaniah 3:5   The Lord does no wrong.

Luke 6:31   Do for others what you want them to do for you.

Colossians 3:17   Do everything for God.

Titus 2:7-8   Be an example of good.

Pretend you're famous and write down how you'd want someone to introduce you when you come on stage to speak. What do you want to be known for? See if you can live up to your expectations.

CHOICES

WHAT CHOICES ARE ALL ABOUT

God says you can choose! You get to make hundreds of choices every day. All of your choices, whether they're little or big, make a difference.

Look at what the Bible has to say about choices:

Deuteronomy 30:15-16   Choose life.

Psalm 119:30   Choose truth.

Proverbs 8:10   Choose God over money.

John 7:17-18   Choose God's will.

John 15:16   God chose you.

1 John 2:15-17   Choosing what's right is always good.

Play a card game where you get to choose, like Old Maid or Go Fish. Think about how you make choices, whether it's which card to choose, what clothes to wear, or who to play with.

CHURCH

WHAT CHURCH IS ALL ABOUT

Wherever people get together to worship God and learn about him, that's church. When you get together with others who love Jesus, you can help each other grow in faith and do more for others in the world who need help.

Look at what the Bible has to say about church:

Matthew 16:15-20   The church has power.

Acts 20:28   Watch over each other in the church.

1 Corinthians 14:12   Use your gifts to help the church.

Ephesians 1:22   Jesus is the head of the church.

Ephesians 5:25-26   Jesus loves his church.

1 Timothy 5:17   Honor those who lead at church.

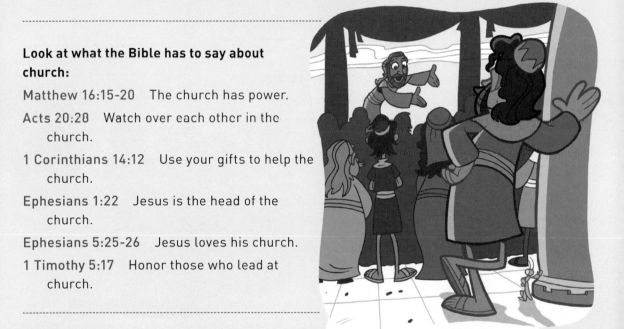

Plan a church service at your house with your family or friends. Decide what you'd like to do and when you want to do it. Include your family in the planning, if you'd like.

CONFESSION

WHAT CONFESSION IS ALL ABOUT

Confession means telling God what you've done when you do something wrong. God already knows what you've done, but he still wants you to talk with him about it. When you talk with him about what you've done wrong, you'll feel better and you'll know what to do next to make things right.

Look at what the Bible has to say about confession:

Nehemiah 9:2-3   Take the time to confess.

Psalm 32:5   Confession leads to forgiveness.

Psalm 51:1-2   God can make us clean.

Daniel 9:4-5   Tell God about everything.

Acts 19:17-18   Knowing Jesus helps us confess.

Romans 14:10-12   You're only responsible for you.

Find a quiet place where you can be alone and have a talk with God. Confess the things you can think of. Tell God how you feel about what you've done. Thank God for understanding and forgiving you.

CONFIDENCE

WHAT CONFIDENCE IS ALL ABOUT

Confidence is how you feel about your actions. If you're sure you did the right thing, you're confident. If you are positive you're right, you're confident.

Look at what the Bible has to say about confidence:

2 Chronicles 32:6-8   Have confidence in God's power.

Psalm 71:5   God gives confidence no matter your age.

Isaiah 32:17   Right living gives confidence.

Jeremiah 17:7-8   Confidence in God pays off.

Ephesians 3:12   Jesus gives confidence.

Hebrews 10:35-36   Keep your confidence.

Stand up as tall as you can and picture God standing right beside you. He is standing there, you know.

God is with you no matter where you go. Think of a time when you're not very sure of yourself. How should you think about yourself, knowing that God is right there with you?

CONFLICT

WHAT CONFLICT IS ALL ABOUT

When you disagree or argue with someone, that's conflict. Fighting with someone is conflict too. There can be good conflict, which helps people become friends again. But most conflict is the bad kind, when people are being proud or foolish.

Look at what the Bible has to say about conflict:

Proverbs 13:10   Pride causes conflict.

Matthew 5:23-26   Settle conflict quickly.

Ephesians 4:26   Don't let anger make you sin.

Colossians 3:8   Get rid of anger.

2 Timothy 2:23   Don't argue.

James 4:1-3   Conflict comes from selfishness.

Hold two magnets close to each other. Depending on which sides you point together, the magnets will either come together or push each other away. Can you think of a conflict you had that pushed another person away from you? Was there any good thing you could have done or said to pull you and the other person closer together?

CONTENTMENT

WHAT CONTENTMENT IS ALL ABOUT

When you're content, you're happy with what you have. You're happy with what you're doing. You're at peace with others around you.

Look at what the Bible has to say about contentment:

Psalm 103:2-5   Think of all God does for you.

Psalm 107:8-9   God gives everything we need.

Proverbs 19:23   God gives contentment.

Philippians 4:11-12   Be content in all things.

1 Timothy 6:6   Godly contentment is good.

Hebrews 13:5   Be content; God is with you.

Find a place where you feel most safe and cozy. Take your favorite toys and stuffed animals, and put on your favorite soft clothes. Then sit in your cozy spot and think about how good it feels to have your favorite things with you. Talk with God about being content with what you have.

COURAGE

WHAT COURAGE IS ALL ABOUT

Courage is being willing to face danger and fear. You can have courage and still be afraid. People of courage know when there is danger, and they're willing to face it. You can have courage when you help someone who others don't. You can have courage when you stand up for what you know is right, even when others may not stand with you.

Look at what the Bible has to say about courage:

Joshua 1:9   Courage comes from God.

Ezra 10:4   Courage gets up and does it.

Acts 4:13   Courage speaks louder than words.

Acts 5:27-29   Courage obeys God over people.

Acts 28:15   Good friends give courage.

2 Timothy 1:7   You have a spirit of power from God.

Stand in front of a mirror and show yourself how you look when you have courage. Try a number of different poses. Do you think you look more like a superhero or a plain old person?

God most often uses people like you to do things that need courage, not superheroes. Next time you need courage, close your eyes and picture yourself in your "courage pose," and then go show your courage.

ETERNAL LIFE

WHAT ETERNAL LIFE IS ALL ABOUT

Living forever in heaven is eternal life. Jesus says there's a place for you in heaven if you know him. Forever is a very, very long time.

Look at what the Bible has to say about eternal life:

Matthew 19:16-24   Riches won't get you to heaven.

Luke 10:25-28   Eternal life comes from loving God.

John 3:16   God sent Jesus to show us the way to heaven.

John 14:1-4   There is a place for you.

1 John 2:24-25   Knowing Jesus brings eternal life.

1 John 5:20   Jesus is eternal life.

Go outside and look up into the sky, away from the sun. How far can you see? Can you see forever? Think about how long eternal life is. Talk to God about your place in heaven.

EVIL

WHAT EVIL IS ALL ABOUT

Evil is everything that is not good. There's plenty of evil in the world, isn't there? Evil causes trouble and brings sadness. God can help us not to do evil and gives us the power to do good.

Look at what the Bible has to say about evil:

Psalm 23:4   Don't fear evil.

Proverbs 8:13   Fear God, hate evil.

Proverbs 29:6   Evil trips you up.

Romans 12:17-21   Overcome evil with good.

1 Thessalonians 5:21-22   Hold on to good, not evil.

1 John 5:18   God keeps us from evil.

Go in a room without windows, like maybe your bathroom. Close the door and turn out the lights. It's not much fun to be in the dark. Evil likes to hang out in dark places. Now, turn on the light. It's much better when the light is on and you can see. Just like light is the opposite of dark, good is the opposite of evil. When you do good, you can turn the light on evil.

FAITH

WHAT FAITH IS ALL ABOUT

Faith is belief in God and what he says in the Bible. Even though you can't see God, you know that God is with you and will help you. When you look at the world around you, you can see that God is at work. Faith is a gift from God and it gives hope.

Look at what the Bible has to say about faith:

Habakkuk 2:4   Good people live by faith.

Matthew 17:20   It takes only a little faith.

Acts 6:8   You can be filled with faith.

Romans 10:17   Faith comes from hearing God's Word.

Hebrews 11:1   Faith is believing what you can't see.

Hebrews 11:6   Faith pleases God.

Sit on your bed and close your eyes. Think about what you can notice without seeing it. What did you find? Is there air to breathe and smells you can smell and sounds you can hear? How is knowing God like knowing there are things like air and smells and sounds? Think of how you can believe that God is with you even without seeing him.

FORGIVENESS

WHAT FORGIVENESS IS ALL ABOUT

Has someone ever owed you something? When you forgive, it's like saying that person doesn't owe you anything anymore. You don't hold anything against them. God gives us forgiveness and doesn't ask for anything in return. It's free. All you have to do is ask for it. You can give forgiveness to others too.

Look at what the Bible has to say about forgiveness:

Psalm 32:1   Forgiveness is a blessing.

Psalm 103:12-13   God's forgiveness separates your sin from you.

Matthew 18:21-22   Forgive often.

Luke 7:47   When you're forgiven much, you love much.

John 20:23   You have the power to forgive.

Romans 4:7-8   Forgiveness erases sin.

Get a pencil and a piece of paper. Write down the things you'd like God to forgive you for. They can be little or big things. Then talk to God and ask him to forgive you. Erase each of the things on your list. That's what God does when you ask for forgiveness.

FREEDOM

WHAT FREEDOM IS ALL ABOUT

Freedom means that you can choose to do what you want. You are free to make lots of decisions every day. You also can be free *from* things, like bad habits or sins that you can't stop by yourself. With God's help, you can find ways to be free from bad things, and you can make good choices every day.

Look at what the Bible has to say about freedom:

Romans 6:15-18   Grace brings freedom from sin.

1 Corinthians 9:19-21   Use freedom to show others about Jesus.

Galatians 5:1   Jesus gives freedom.

Galatians 5:13   Use freedom to serve.

James 1:25   God's law gives freedom.

1 Peter 2:16   Use freedom rightly.

Go in your bedroom and close the door. With the door closed, you're not free to go anywhere. When you open the door, you can go lots of places. As you stand in your doorway, think about the freedom God has given you to make decisions. Think about a time when he freed you from a bad habit or helped you decide to do something good, not bad. Thank him for giving you so much freedom.

FRIENDSHIP

WHAT FRIENDSHIP IS ALL ABOUT

How you treat your friends and get along with them is friendship. You probably have one or two close friends and then others who are not so close. There are lots of different kinds of friends: church friends, neighbor friends, school friends, sports friends. There's also friendship with God.

Look at what the Bible has to say about friendship:

Genesis 5:22-24   Walk with God.

Proverbs 17:17   Friends love all the time.

Proverbs 27:10   Take care of your friends.

Ecclesiastes 4:10   Friends help each other.

John 15:13-15   Jesus calls you friend.

James 2:23   Believe God and be his friend.

Draw a picture of you and your best friend. Make a list of the things you do together that make you friends. Thank God for your friend and for the friendship you can have with God too.

GIVING

WHAT GIVING IS ALL ABOUT

Giving has to do with being generous and unselfish. When you give, you take something that is yours and let someone else have it. You can give love, money, gifts, even help and kind words. God has lots to say about giving. He gives us much more than we can ever give away.

Look at what the Bible has to say about giving:

Deuteronomy 16:17   Give as you are able.

1 Chronicles 16:29   Give God the glory.

Psalm 107:21   Give thanks always.

Luke 6:30   Give to whoever asks.

Acts 20:35   It's better to give than to receive.

1 Timothy 4:15   Give it your all.

Think about all the things you have to give. It could be a smile, a kind word, help with chores, money you earn, a picture you draw, or something you make. God has given you many gifts. Think of how you can give something away today. Give it with a smile and a happy heart.

GRACE

WHAT GRACE IS ALL ABOUT

Grace comes from God and from other people. Grace is forgiveness and love when we don't deserve it. God gives grace freely if we're willing to take it. It's a gift.

Look at what the Bible has to say about grace:

John 1:16-17   Grace comes from Jesus.

Romans 4:16   Grace is a promise.

1 Corinthians 15:10   God's grace grows us.

2 Corinthians 12:9   God's grace is all we
    need.

Ephesians 2:5   God's grace gives life.

Ephesians 3:7   God's grace is a gift.

Find a small, empty box and wrap it in fun paper and then write the word *grace* on it in big letters. Put it where you'll be reminded of God's gift of grace for you.

HELPING

WHAT HELPING IS ALL ABOUT

Helping means seeing what needs to be done and doing it. Sometimes people ask for help, sometimes they don't, but people appreciate it when you volunteer to help.

Look at what the Bible has to say about helping:

Psalm 10:12   Remember those who need help.

Psalm 121:1-4   God will help you.

1 Corinthians 12:28   Helping is a gift from God.

2 Corinthians 9:1-3   Be known as a helper.

Ephesians 6:7   Serve with your heart.

1 Thessalonians 5:14   Help the weak.

Look around and find someone you can help. Maybe your mom needs help with the dishes or your little brother needs help cleaning his room. Find a way to be helpful today.

HONESTY

WHAT HONESTY IS ALL ABOUT

Honesty doesn't hide anything. It means that you tell the truth and mean it. Sometimes it's hard to be honest, but it's always the right thing to do. The Bible is full of honest truth, the kind that never changes, whether others believe it or not.

Look at what the Bible says about honesty:

Leviticus 19:36-37   The Lord desires honesty.

2 Kings 12:15   Honesty can be trusted.

Psalm 57:10   Honesty stands tall.

Psalm 86:11   Walk in truth.

Proverbs 12:19   Honesty lasts a long time.

Ephesians 4:14-15   Honesty helps us grow up right.

There are many times when we are tempted to be less than honest. Often it's easy not to say anything at all or to stretch the truth just a little. We need to be honest, whether anyone will notice or not. Choose to be completely honest until tomorrow at this same time. Ask Jesus to help you make all the right and honest choices. See if you can do it.

HOPE

WHAT HOPE IS ALL ABOUT

Hope is looking forward to good things, trusting that they will happen. Hope is when you trust God because he knows best. God's promises also give lots of hope. He says that he will always take care of you. He also says he has a good life planned for you and a place ready for you in heaven. What great things to hope for!

Look at what the Bible has to say about hope:

Jeremiah 29:11   There is a hope and a plan for you.

Romans 8:23-25   Hope means waiting.

Romans 12:12   Be joyful in hope.

Colossians 1:4-5   Hope brings love.

1 Thessalonians 1:3   Hope gets you through.

1 Timothy 1:1   Jesus is our hope.

Set your favorite toy out where you can see it. Now see if you can wait to play with it until tomorrow. Hope is like that—waiting for something really great and knowing it will happen.

HUMILITY

WHAT HUMILITY IS ALL ABOUT

When you have humility, you know that you can't do anything without God's help. You give credit and honor to others instead of keeping it for yourself. When you're humble, you don't need lots of pats on the back for doing things.

Look at what the Bible has to say about humility:

Psalm 34:2-3   The humble brag on God.

Psalm 149:4   God makes the humble beautiful.

Proverbs 22:4   Humility leads to honor and riches.

Zephaniah 2:3   Seeking humility hides you from God's anger.

Romans 12:16   Hang out with the humble.

1 Peter 5:5-7   You should wear humility like clothes.

Look around for a way to help someone, and then do it without letting them know—ever. How does it feel to do something and not get the credit for it? God can give you the strength to do lots of things. It'll be reward enough to know that God knows you did it with his help. Look for ways to be humble at school and when you're playing sports too.

JOY

WHAT JOY IS ALL ABOUT

Joy is different from being happy. You can be happy when you get lots of presents on your birthday. But happiness can disappear when your new toy breaks or a friend gets mad at you. Joy is bigger than being happy. It's a good feeling, but it's also knowing that God loves you no matter what. Joy is something that isn't changed by what is happening around you.

Look at what the Bible has to say about joy:

Nehemiah 8:10   Joy from God gives strength.

Psalm 16:11   God's presence brings joy.

Psalm 95:1-7   Joy leads to worship.

Psalm 126:5-6   Joy will come after sadness.

Luke 2:10   Jesus brings joy.

Romans 15:13   God fills you with joy.

Think about all the things that give you joy. Look at your hands and think about how they work. Think about how your brain thinks and your eyes see. Plan a party with your family where you'll each have a chance to thank God for the things that give you joy. Think of how you can share your joy with others too.

LEARNING

WHAT LEARNING IS ALL ABOUT

Learning is putting information into your brain. Sometimes you do it by trying things; sometimes you do it by reading or talking. Learning always takes practice.

Look at what the Bible has to say about learning:

Deuteronomy 5:1   Learn the commandments.

Proverbs 9:9   Add to your learning.

Isaiah 1:17   Learn to do right.

Matthew 11:29   Learn from Jesus.

Philippians 4:11   Learn to be content.

2 Timothy 3:14   Use what you've learned.

Think of one thing you'd like to learn—and learn it. Maybe it's a new soccer kick or a song on the piano or a favorite Scripture verse. Think about how you like to learn, and thank God for giving you your brain and the ability to learn.

LISTENING

WHAT LISTENING IS ALL ABOUT

Listening is more than hearing. Hearing is what your ears do. Listening is using your brain along with your ears. It's paying attention to what your ears are hearing.

Look at what the Bible has to say about listening:

Deuteronomy 30:20   Listen to God.

Proverbs 1:5   Listen and learn.

Proverbs 8:33   Listen and be wise.

James 1:19   Be quick to listen.

James 1:22   Listen and then do.

1 John 5:14-15   God listens.

Find a place to sit outside where you can listen. Sit very still and listen for at least ten different things. Listen for a breeze in the air, the soft sounds of birds, squirrels rustling in leaves, or bugs flying around. Listen for noises close by and far away. Then think about what it's like to listen to God.

LOVE

WHAT LOVE IS ALL ABOUT

Love is a deep and unchanging feeling toward another. It means that you consider them most important and will take care of them and do good things for them.

Look at what the Bible has to say about love:

Matthew 5:44   Love your enemies.

Mark 12:30   Love God with all you've got.

1 Corinthians 13:4-8   Love is lots of things.

1 Corinthians 13:13   Love is the best.

1 John 4:7-12   Love comes from God.

1 John 4:19-21   God loved you first.

Look at the picture on this page and see how many different ways people are showing love. How do you show love to your family, to your friends, to your neighbors, to God?

MERCY

WHAT MERCY IS ALL ABOUT

Mercy is showing love and forgiveness for others in a tender and caring way because they need it. God shows you mercy and you can show mercy to others.

Look at what the Bible has to say about mercy:

Isaiah 63:9   God's love and mercy saves us.

Daniel 9:18   God has great mercy.

Hosea 6:6   God wants mercy not sacrifice.

Micah 6:8   Love mercy.

Luke 1:50   God's mercy is for those who honor him.

Jude 1:21-23   Show mercy to others.

Lie down on the floor, looking at the ceiling. Ask your mom or dad to help you up. Mercy is like that. Mercy helps people up when they're down. Think about people who need your help.

MONEY

WHAT MONEY IS ALL ABOUT

Money is how we pay for things. Money can be used to pay for lots of good things, like food and clothes and birthday presents. But if we love money too much, always wanting more and more, we can forget about God. Then we start doing wrong things with money, like stealing it or using it to make ourselves feel important.

Look at what the Bible has to say about money:

Proverbs 13:11   Use money wisely.

Ecclesiastes 5:10   If you love money, you never have enough.

Matthew 6:24   You can't serve God and money.

1 Corinthians 16:2   Set money aside.

1 Timothy 6:10   Loving money causes problems.

1 Peter 5:2   Serve others instead of loving money.

Think of all of the good things you can use money for. Decide on one of those good things you'd like to do. Find a little jar or bowl and set it in your room. As often as you can, put coins in your jar and see if you can fill it up. When it's full, use it to do the good thing you thought of.

OBEDIENCE

WHAT OBEDIENCE IS ALL ABOUT

Obedience means that you obey when you're asked to do something. Lots of people ask you to do things: your mom and dad, your teacher, the police, your brothers and sisters, and others. God asks you to do things too. Learning to obey is part of growing up. When you obey, others know they can trust you.

Look at what the Bible has to say about obedience:

Genesis 27:8   Obey by doing what God says.

Exodus 19:5   Those who obey are God's treasures.

Deuteronomy 11:13-15   Obedience leads to riches.

Deuteronomy 12:28   Obey right away and it will be well.

Ephesians 6:1-3   Obeying parents is right.

Colossians 3:20-24   Obey. You're doing it for God.

Did you clean your room and take out the trash? Were you asked to feed the dog or cat? If so, give yourself a pat on the back. If you forgot, go do it and then give yourself a pat on the back. See if you can do your chores without being reminded. If you can, you're showing that you're growing up.

PARENTS

WHAT PARENTS ARE ALL ABOUT

Your mom and dad are your parents. Sometimes God sends extra adults to be your parents too. Parents are sent by God to love you and look out for you while you grow up.

Look at what the Bible has to say about parents:

Exodus 20:12   Honor your parents.

Proverbs 10:1   Wise children bring joy to their parents.

Proverbs 19:14   Parents pass on wealth.

Proverbs 23:22   Listen to your parents.

Ephesians 6:1-3   Obey your parents.

1 Timothy 5:4   Repay your parents.

Write a note to your parents, telling them what they're doing right. If you don't want to write it down, just go tell them. This is a good way to honor your parents.

PRAISE

WHAT PRAISE IS ALL ABOUT

Praise is when you look for all of the good in someone and tell them about it. God deserves our praise because he does so many good things.

Look at what the Bible has to say about praise:

Psalm 34:1   Praise God always.

Psalm 89:5   Even heaven praises God.

Psalm 105:1-5   Tell everyone how wonderful God is.

Psalm 139:14   Praise God for making you.

Psalm 147:1   It's good to praise God.

Psalm 150:6   Everything praises God.

Fans cheer for their team when they're doing a good job. When you think about all the wonderful things God has done for you, do you feel like cheering? Then go ahead and cheer! That's praise.

PRAYER

WHAT PRAYER IS ALL ABOUT

Prayer is talking to God. We may thank him, praise him, ask him for help, tell him we love him, or just listen to him—and it's all prayer. Prayer is a gift from God. He hears our prayers and answers them.

Look at what the Bible says about prayer:

Exodus 33:13-14   Pray for direction and favor.

1 Chronicles 16:11   Always pray.

Luke 6:28   Pray for those who mistreat you.

Luke 11:2-4   Here's a way to pray.

James 5:13   Pray when you're hurting.

James 5:16   Pray for healing.

God wants to talk with you all the time. Take a minute right now to tell God thanks for three things. Then go do something you enjoy doing, like shooting hoops or jumping rope. For every basket you make or rope you jump, tell God thanks for something more. See how much you can thank God for. See if you can pray when you're kicking a soccer ball or even doing your chores. Make it a habit to talk to God lots of times every day.

PRIORITIES

WHAT PRIORITIES ARE ALL ABOUT

What you think is most important is your priority. Whatever you choose to spend your free time doing, that's your priority. Maybe you have more than one priority, like friends and video games and reading.

Look at what the Bible has to say about priorities:

Joshua 24:15   Make God a priority.

Psalm 27:4-5   Make church a priority.

Psalm 34:10   Godly priorities are full of good things.

Proverbs 12:26   Make good friends a priority.

Luke 12:29-31   Put God first, and the rest follows.

1 Corinthians 10:24   Make others a priority.

Make a list of the things you do when you're not at school, sleeping, or doing what adults ask you to do. Then make a star next to each one for each hour you spend doing it. What do you spend the most time on? Is there anything you want to do less, or more? Try it. Spend the time you want on what's important and stop spending time on something less important to you.

PROMISES

WHAT PROMISES ARE ALL ABOUT

A promise means you'll do what you say, no matter what. A promise is a serious thing and isn't meant to be broken. When God makes a promise, he keeps it.

Look at what the Bible has to say about promises:

Numbers 10:29   God's promises are good.

Psalm 119:148   Think about God's promises.

Acts 2:33   God promises the Holy Spirit.

2 Corinthians 1:20-22   God's promise is through Jesus.

Hebrews 10:23   God keeps his promises.

2 Peter 1:4   God's promises are great.

Make a list of any promises that you have made. Then find a rock for each promise on your list. A rock is like a promise because it's not easily broken. Look around outside and find other things that remind you of a promise. Make a promise collection and tell your mom or dad about your collection.

PURITY

WHAT PURITY IS ALL ABOUT

Purity is being clean and simple. Being pure is filling your mind with so many good things that there's no room for the bad stuff. Being pure means that you do what's right whether anyone is looking or not.

Look at what the Bible has to say about purity:

2 Samuel 22:27   God shows his purity to those who are pure.

Proverbs 15:26   Purity pleases God.

Proverbs 20:11   Children are known by their purity.

Matthew 5:8   Pure people see God.

Philippians 4:8   Think about purity all the time.

1 Timothy 4:12   Be an example of purity for others.

With permission, fix your favorite snack. Enjoy every bite of it. That's how God feels about you when you keep yourself pure. When you do the right things and think the right thoughts, that pleases God more than the best snack in the world.

REPENTANCE

WHAT REPENTANCE IS ALL ABOUT

Repentance is changing your mind. It means stopping what you're doing, turning around, and going in a new direction. When you say the wrong thing, disobey your parents, or do less than your best at school, you need to repent. To repent, you tell God you're sorry and don't want to do that thing anymore. When you repent, God promises to forgive you and show you new ways that are better—and sometimes more fun!

Look at what the Bible says about repentance:

Jeremiah 25:5   Repent from evil.

Luke 15:7   Heaven celebrates those who repent.

Acts 3:19-20   Repenting leads to good feelings.

Acts 17:30   God wants you to repent.

2 Peter 3:9   You are supposed to repent.

Revelation 3:19   Repent as quickly as possible.

Think about something in your life that you need to stop doing. Walk in one direction while you talk to God about it. Then turn and walk in the other direction while you listen for God to help you go in a better direction, away from what you want to stop doing. Walk back and forth as many times as you need to while you're talking with God. Then go and use what you hear to help you do the right thing.

RESPECT

WHAT RESPECT IS ALL ABOUT

Respect is when you show honor to others because of who they are. You show respect to those you look up to. Parents, teachers, pastors, grandparents—they're all people you respect. These people are older and wiser than you. Another word for respect is honor. Showing respect or honor is one way to show love.

Look at what the Bible has to say about respect:

Leviticus 19:32   Offer respect to the elderly.

Deuteronomy 5:16   Respect your parents.

Proverbs 3:9-10   Honor God.

Proverbs 4:7-8   Wisdom brings respect.

John 5:23   Honor Jesus like the Father.

Romans 13:7   Offer respect when it's due.

In the military, soldiers salute to show respect. In some countries, people bow to show respect. Think of something special you can do to show respect, like a special salute, saying "sir" or "ma'am," or something else. Make sure it's something that others will also know is showing respect. Use it to show your parents you respect them. Use it to show your grandparents or your friends you respect them. Tell them what you're doing and why. They'll be pleased to know how you feel about them—and to see a reminder of it.

SADNESS

WHAT SADNESS IS ALL ABOUT

Sadness is the opposite of happiness. Sometimes you cry; sometimes your throat or your stomach hurts. *Sorrow* and *grief* are two words that also mean sadness.

Look at what the Bible has to say about sadness:

Psalm 10:14   God sees our sadness.

Proverbs 14:13   You can be happy and sad at the same time.

Isaiah 60:20   Sadness will end.

John 16:20   Sadness will turn to joy.

Romans 8:26-27   The Holy Spirit helps us pray when we're sad.

2 Corinthians 7:10   Godly sadness brings repentance.

Pretend you're flying. Think about what it might feel like to fly and what you might see. When you're sad, you can pretend you're flying. You can look down on what makes you sad and imagine God holding you up with his big hands.

SIN

WHAT SIN IS ALL ABOUT

Sin is anything you think or do or say that doesn't please God. Sins come in all different shapes and sizes, but they're all the same to God.

Look at what the Bible has to say about sin:

Numbers 5:5-7   You must confess your sin.

Psalm 51:3-4   Your sins are against God.

Romans 3:23   Everyone has sinned.

Romans 5:6-8   Jesus died for your sins.

Romans 6:11-14   Don't let sin rule you.

1 John 1:8-10   Jesus will forgive your sins.

Find a piece of scratch paper and a wastebasket. Think of one thing you've done or thought or said that didn't please God. Tear off a piece of the paper while you're telling God about it. Then throw the piece away. That's what God does when you tell him about your sins; he throws them away and forgets about them.

SUBMISSION

WHAT SUBMISSION IS ALL ABOUT

Submission is letting those who love you be your boss. When you submit to God by doing what he asks, you let him be the boss of you. It doesn't sound like much fun, but when you submit to God, things are actually lots easier! God helps you make good choices and helps you have joy, even when you have to do hard things.

Look at what the Bible has to say about submission:

Romans 13:1-7   Submit to your country's laws.

Ephesians 5:21   Submit to each other as Christians.

Hebrews 12:9-10   Submit even in discipline.

Hebrews 13:17   Submit to your leaders.

James 3:17   Heavenly wisdom submits.

James 4:7   Submit to God.

Another way of thinking about submission is to think of putting yourself under someone else. Find a safe place where you can sit under something, like under a blanket or table, even under a tree. Think about how it feels to sit under it. Submission can make you feel safe. Submitting to God will help you make better choices and help you feel his presence with you.

THANKFULNESS

WHAT THANKFULNESS IS ALL ABOUT

Thankfulness is being filled up with gladness about the good things in your life. How many things are you thankful for? Are you thankful for your family and friends? Are you thankful for your clothes and food? Are you thankful for the place where you live and your bed to sleep in? When you can name lots of things you're happy about, you're thankful!

Look at what the Bible has to say about thankfulness:

Psalm 100:1-5   Thank God for all his goodness.

Daniel 2:23   Thank God for wisdom.

Philippians 1:3-6   Be thankful that God finishes what he starts.

Colossians 3:15   Thankfulness and peace go together.

1 Timothy 1:12   Be thankful for strength to serve.

Philemon 1:4-6   Be thankful for every good thing.

Find a ball and go outside, or use a balloon and stay inside. Think of all of the things you're thankful for. Every time you think of something, toss the ball or balloon up in the air and then catch it. See how long you can keep going without repeating anything you're thankful for. Can you think of fifteen? How about fifty?

THOUGHTS

WHAT THOUGHTS ARE ALL ABOUT

You are what you think. What you become is decided by what you think too. Because what you think about can make you act certain ways, what you think about is very important. What you put in your brain is the only stuff that you'll think about. You can't think about anything you haven't put into your brain.

Look at what the Bible has to say about your thoughts:

Psalm 63:6-8   Think about God when you're going to bed.

Psalm 77:11-12   Remember what God has done.

Psalm 94:11   God knows our thoughts.

Psalm 119:15-16   Think about God's ways.

Hebrews 3:1-2   Think about Jesus.

2 Peter 3:1   Good friends help you think well.

Find a plastic jar or cup and fill it with things you find in your room. Look at what's in there. How did the stuff get there? Is there anything in there that you're surprised about? Everything that's in there, you put there. Set your cup or jar where you can see it as a reminder that you are in charge of what goes in your brain too.

TRUST

WHAT TRUST IS ALL ABOUT

When people trust you, they believe you will do what you say. You trust others when they keep their word. Trust is something that's earned over time, and it's very important.

Look at what the Bible has to say about trust:

Psalm 9:10   You can trust God to be with you.

Psalm 56:3-4   Trust God when you're afraid.

Psalm 119:42   Trust God's Word.

Daniel 6:3-4   Be known as someone to be trusted.

Luke 19:12-26   Grow your trust.

1 Timothy 6:17-19   Trust God, not money.

Remember a time when you told a friend a secret, and he or she promised not to tell. If your friend told anyway, you probably won't trust him or her with another secret. But if your friend was trustworthy and didn't tell, what a great friend! God is like that. The more you get to know him, the more you'll see that his Word can always be trusted.

TRUTH

WHAT TRUTH IS ALL ABOUT

Truth is fact. Truth is honest. Truth is what is real. God has told us lots of truth in his Word, the Bible. For instance, it's always true that he loves us and that he will never leave us.

Look at what the Bible has to say about truth:

Psalm 26:3   Walk in God's truth.

Psalm 33:4   God's Word is true.

Proverbs 16:13   Truth is valuable.

Zechariah 8:16   Tell the truth.

John 8:31-32   Jesus' truth sets you free.

John 14:6   Jesus is truth.

Lie down with your feet against a wall and put something at the top of your head, like a book. Now get up and measure how tall you are using a ruler or even a shoe. Take the measure five more times to make sure you're right. What other things are you sure about? Those are truths.

WISDOM

WHAT WISDOM IS ALL ABOUT

Wisdom is lots more than knowing things. It's making good choices and thinking things through. Wisdom is doing what's right and listening to good advice. Being smart is good; being wise is even better!

Look at what the Bible has to say about wisdom:

Exodus 31:3-4   Wisdom is artistic.

Deuteronomy 4:5-6   Wisdom obeys God's Word.

2 Chronicles 1:11-12   Wisdom comes before riches and honor.

Psalm 90:12   Wisdom makes good use of time.

Proverbs 4:5-6   Get wisdom more than anything.

Proverbs 29:3   Wise children make parents proud.

Who is the wisest person you know? Go and tell that person you think he or she is wise, and then ask that wise person to help you be wise too. Read one Scripture every morning from the book of Proverbs in your Bible. It's full of wise things.

_____

(Write your own word here)

WHAT _____ IS ALL ABOUT
(Describe the word, give a definition, etc.)

_____

_____

_____

_____

_____

Write 4-6 Bible passages that talk about the word here:

_____

_____

_____

_____

_____

How can you live out the truth of this word today?

_____

_____

_____

_____

_____
(Write your own word here)

WHAT _____ IS ALL ABOUT
(Describe the word, give a definition, etc.)

_____

_____

_____

_____

_____

_____

Write 4-6 Bible passages that talk about the word here:

_____

_____

_____

_____

_____

_____

How can you live out the truth of this word today?

_____

_____

_____

_____

_____
(Write your own word here)

WHAT _____ IS ALL ABOUT
(Describe the word, give a definition, etc.)

_____
_____
_____
_____
_____

Write 4-6 Bible passages that talk about the word here:

_____
_____
_____
_____
_____
_____

How can you live out the truth of this word today?

_____
_____
_____
_____

_____
(Write your own word here)

WHAT _____ IS ALL ABOUT
(Describe the word, give a definition, etc.)

_____

_____

_____

_____

_____

_____

Write 4-6 Bible passages that talk about the word here:

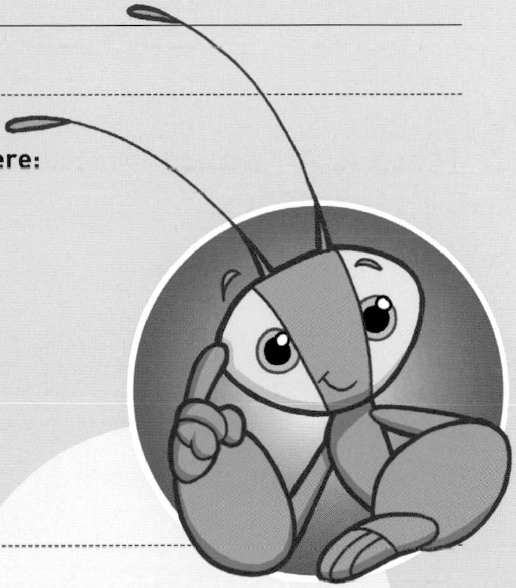

_____

_____

_____

_____

_____

How can you live out the truth of this word today?

_____

_____

_____

_____
(Write your own word here)

WHAT _____ IS ALL ABOUT
(Describe the word, give a definition, etc.)

_____

_____

_____

_____

_____

- -

Write 4-6 Bible passages that talk about the word here:

How can you live out the truth of this word today?

_____

_____

_____

_____

(Write your own word here)
_____

WHAT _____ IS ALL ABOUT
(Describe the word, give a definition, etc.)

_____

_____

_____

_____

_____

Write 4-6 Bible passages that talk about the word here:

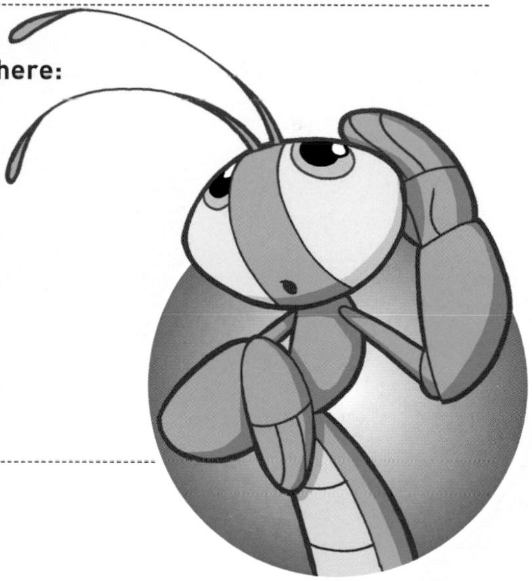

_____

_____

_____

_____

_____

How can you live out the truth of this word today?

_____

_____

_____

_____

ABOUT THE AUTHOR

Jon Nappa has worked in television and motion pictures for more than twenty years. His work as a screenwriter earned him an invitation to meet with George Lucas at Skywalker Ranch. In addition to writing inspirational novels, Jon spearheads a Media-with-a-Mission franchise designed to inspire children to intentionally navigate the Bible on their own. He lives with his wife and four children in North Carolina.

Rob Corley and **Tom Bancroft** have over thirty years of combined experience in the animation industry, most of which was for Walt Disney Feature animation. While at Disney, the partners had the opportunity to contribute animation on ten animated feature films, five animated shorts, and numerous special projects and commercials. Some of the classic films include *Beauty and the Beast*, *The Lion King*, *Aladdin*, *Mulan*, *Lilo and Stitch*, and *Brother Bear*. Bancroft was also a character designer and director for Big Idea Productions, makers of the family-friendly *Veggie Tales* video series.

They are partners in Funnypages Productions, LLC, a company that provides illustration, character design, and artistic animation development. Funnypages Productions has also developed many original properties for film and television and illustrated over twenty-five children's books. They and their families live in Nashville, Tennessee. For more information, see www.funnypagesprod.com.

SCRIPTURE INDEX

(Note: Page reference numbers are in orange.)

TOPICAL INDEX

(**Note:** Page reference numbers are in orange.)

MY FIRST MESSAGE PRODUCTS

This mini-book series brings all the fun and wonder of *My First Message* into selected stories of the Bible. The enclosed CDs help kids enjoy read-along narration and catchy, upbeat tunes. All of which makes Bible learning feel like, well, kid stuff.

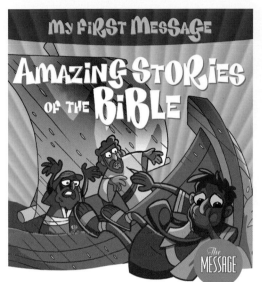

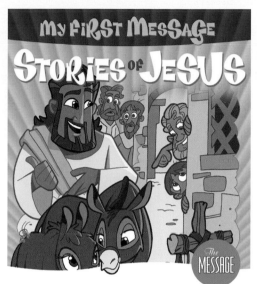

AMAZING STORIES OF THE BIBLE

- David and Goliath
- Daniel in the Lions' Den
- Bread and Fish for All
- Jonah and the Huge Fish

MY FIRST MESSAGE STORIES OF JESUS

- Jesus Is Baptized
- Jesus Calms the Sea
- The Triumphal Entry and Jesus in the Temple
- Jesus Washes the Disciples' Feet

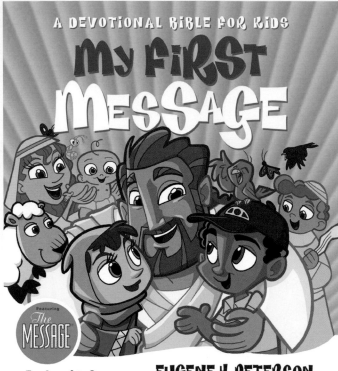

MY FIRST MESSAGE BIBLE

Much more than a storybook, *My First Message* is an easy and fun way for parents to teach their children about God's Word and learn a lifelong devotional method.

Features include:

- A unique devotional Bible for children ages 4 to 8
- Lively illustrations
- Short lessons for small attention spans
- Fun activities for parents and children

Visit your local Christian bookstore,
call NavPress at 1-800-366-7788, or log on to www.NavPress.com to purchase.
To locate a Christian bookstore near you,
call 1-800-991-7747.

NAVPRESS ®